Beauty Mark

Beauty Mark

A Verse Novel of Marilyn Monroe

CAROLE BOSTON WEATHERFORD

CANDLEWICK PRESS

Copyright © 2020 by Carole Boston Weatherford

First edition 2020

Library of Congress Catalog Card Number pending
ISBN 978-1-5362-0629-6

20 21 22 23 24 25 LEO 10 9 8 7 6 5 4 3 2 1

Printed in Heshan, Guangdong, China

This book was typeset in Minion Pro.

Candlewick Press
99 Dover Street
Somerville, Massachusetts 02144

www.candlewick.com

A JUNIOR LIBRARY GUILD SELECTION

*For anyone who's ever been disrespected,
mistreated, underestimated, or misunderstood.
Let your star shine.*

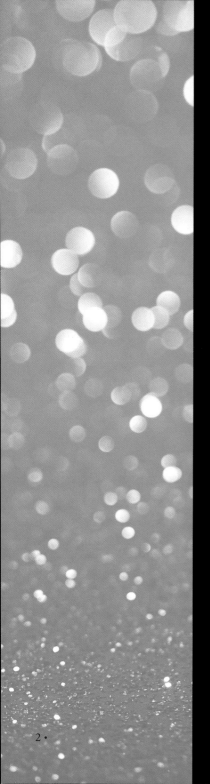

Stand Still

I am nude —
about to be sewn into the dress
that I paid Oscar winner Jean Louis
twelve thousand dollars to design.
The sequined second skin I will wear
to sing "Happy Birthday"
to Jack Kennedy, the president.
I was coiffed by the same beautician
who does First Lady Jackie Kennedy's hai
Nothing in my Norma Jeane beginnings
pointed toward this moment.

This is no accident, though.
I rehearsed this song
until it became my breath.
I exhale memory after memory
while a stylist stitches me into history.
For hours, I stand perfectly still
as my shimmery silhouette takes shape.
I am silvery as a movie screen.
Hollywood's old guard scoffed
that I could not act my way
out of a paper bag.

What did they know?

Mom Never Smiled

After I was born, June 1, my mother
first held me with her eyes closed,
not gazing at my face
but plunging into darkness.
She was so low that she couldn't
care for herself, let alone a baby.
As her mother, Della, said,
She needs to get her mind right first.

When I was newborn, Della stuck around
a few days and made my mother promise
to entrust me to a neighbor
across the street — Ida Bolender.
After Della left, my mom's friend Grace
stayed with me once while Mom bought groceries.
When Mom got back, she accused Grace of poisoning me.
Then Mom stabbed Grace with a kitchen knife.

By June 13, I was in Ida Bolender's arms.
At the time, it was for the best.

Age Three

This may be my earliest recollection.
I am screaming because my mother, Gladys,
has stuffed me in a military duffel bag.

Her mother, Della, had died two years earlier.
My mother and grandmother both got the blues,
heard voices, and leaned on each other.

With Della gone, Gladys had only the voices
and they offered neither comfort nor peace.
They were telling her to get her child.

Now, after three years of paying the Bolenders
five dollars a week to keep me because she could not,
my mother has come to claim me.

She snatches me from my foster family,
the only home I know.
But Ida Bolender will not let me go.

There is a tug-of-war between my two mothers.
The duffel bag rips open.
I tumble to the ground yelling, *Mommy!*

Ida scoops me up, runs inside, and locks the door.

Della

I'm not sure who was sicker,
my mother, Gladys, or my grandmother, Della.
When I was just a year old,
Della got it in her head that I was dead
and no one had told my blood relatives.
She banged on the Bolenders' door,
but Ida didn't open it. So Della poked her elbow
through the glass and let herself in.
Then she and Ida had words.

To calm Della down, Ida let her see
that I was asleep in my crib.
It must have been hot that day,
because Ida left the room
to get Della a drink of water.
When Ida returned, she caught Della
trying to smother me with a pillow.
Ida and Wayne Bolender called the police.
The very thought still takes my breath away.

Della Monroe and Gladys Baker:
Like Mother, Like Daughter

Both petite beauties
who suffered mood swings,
had crying spells and baby blues.
Both heard voices
that one told the other were not real.
Both were easy, slept around,
married alcoholics.
Had multiple husbands
and failed marriages,
and gave up children:
Uncle Martin and me.

Foster Care

In the Bolenders' devout Baptist household,
I was one of several foster children.
But they loved me, wanted to adopt me.
My mother, Gladys, would not hear of that.

Ida Bolender was a self-righteous taskmaster,
and her husband, Wayne, a hardworking mailman.
They were churchgoers, not moviegoers.
My foster parents grew vegetables
and raised chickens, goats, and sometimes rabbits.
They even had lemon and fig trees.

We rode in a Ford Model T, sang songs,
solved riddles, and listened to Daddy's stories.
Ida sewed all my dresses. I tried her patience
playing in dirt. We children passed rainy days
in the fort under our dining room table;
ate lunch there too.

Usually five foster children,
but always enough love to go around.
Ida wanted me to be strong like her.

The Only Father I Ever Knew:
Wayne Bolender

My foster father, Wayne Bolender, carried mail.
His heart was big as his leather delivery bag.
He had a wiry frame and gray eyes
and wore tortoiseshell horn-rim glasses.
Stalwart as the Postal Service itself,
he could find joy in any circumstance.
Like Ida, he was a devout Baptist.
On a printing press in the house,
he made prayer cards for the church.
That was his way of glorifying the Lord.

The Meaning of Mama

Don't call me Mama,
said Ida Bolender, my foster mother,
explaining that we were not kin.
You're old enough to know better.
You just board here, she said,
adding that my mother would be visiting the next day.
Call her Mama if you want.

Gladys never kissed me
or held me or had much to say to me,
but I obeyed my foster mother.
Hello, Mama, I said.
Gladys just stared.
At least I knew who she was.

When I visited the rooming house
where she lived, I hid in the closet for hours.
Frightened.
As I lay in bed at night turning the pages of a book,
she'd say, *Don't make so much noise, Norma.*
The sound made her nervous.

Mama had plenty to grieve about.
Her father and grandmother both died
in mental hospitals, and her brother
killed himself. Her unhappy childhood ended

at age fifteen when she married a man twelve years older.
She had two children by Jasper Baker
and two concussions at his hand
before coming home early from work
and catching him in bed with another woman.

None of the silent negatives she spliced
as a film cutter for a movie studio
prepared Gladys for the scene that day
or for the fallout.
After a big fight, Jasper left Gladys —
but not for good, not without the children.
Mama was so down that she didn't see him
sneak back and kidnap her two babies.
She spent many months and all her savings
on a hunt that led to Kentucky.
She hitchhiked there.
Jasper had a new wife and a fine home.
And her children had a shot at happiness.
Mama didn't have the heart to face them,
believing they were better off without her.
By the time I was born, she was claiming
that her two older children were dead.
She practiced the lie so often,
she may have come to believe it.

Mama's Dream House

I was in the kitchen when my mother dropped by.
She didn't say a word
and I went right on washing dishes.
When I looked back at her,
she broke her silence.
I'm going to build us a white house one day,
she promised. *We'll even have a backyard.*
She painted a heartwarming picture.
But before Mama could keep her promise,
a breakdown sent her to the mental hospital.
Through torment and treatment,
that dream house anchored her.

Tippy

If only Tippy hadn't barked so much.
If only our neighbor had been a dog lover.
If only the dog had not run in front of a car.
If only Ida hadn't removed the carcass
from the street to the driveway
for her husband to discard.
If only my foster father had gotten home
and buried the dog before I saw it.
If only I'd believed Ida Bolender's story.
If only I had not insisted that the mean neighbor
had cut Tippy in half with a hoe.
If only I hadn't cried for two days
over the dog's death.
If only Ida had been able to console me,
she might not have given up on raising me.
If only I had been able to stay with the Bolenders.

Reunion

I was so upset over losing Tippy
that I stopped crying only in my sleep.
Mama had been telling Ida
that she wanted me back.
Now she would get her wish.
My foster mother, Ida, called her to come for me.
The next day, Ida announced that Mama
would be taking me home with her.
My foster brothers and sisters sobbed.
But I am home, I pleaded.

Ida said I could come back anytime,
that she'd always be there for me.
We'll always love you, she promised.
Before long, a horn tooted.
Mama didn't even get out of the car.
I climbed in back and rode off
with a woman I barely knew.
I was leaving the only parents I ever loved.
Out my window, Ida faded like a mirage.

The Bolenders were behind me.

Aunt Grace

At the Bolenders' Baptist church, I learned
that God promised grace to believers.
Mama's Grace was coworker, best friend, and angel.
Aunt Grace was a bottle-blond flapper
who wanted to be on-screen like her idol
Jean Harlow. But Grace chose dreaming
of being an actress over working to become one.
Still, her allure drew every eye her way.
Grace was as fierce as Mama was fretful,
as optimistic as Mama was morose.
Grace was the sun over the horizon.
Mama was the moon,
waxing and waning between dark moods.
Mama needed Grace,
and Grace took charge, telling Mama
to show more skin, buy a new wardrobe,
and dye her mousy-brown hair red.
Grace even corrected Mama's grammar.
Grace liked to lend advice and solve problems.
Mama offered plenty of opportunities for both.
With my grandmother Della gone,
Mama leaned on Grace.
The two of them shared a tiny apartment.
I made three.

Sundays

Mom and I were not regular churchgoers,
but when we went, I was in heaven.
The songs and sacraments held me in a trance.
Around noon, we'd head home for a chicken lunch
with Mama's friends. Afterward, we strolled
past fancy storefronts, window-shopping.
Wishing was all we could afford.
On our walks, I'd see other children
holding hands with their moms and dads.
I wanted a daddy to talk to, play with, and hug.
Mom loved me, but she was sad and lonely too.
I suppose she couldn't help it.

My First Happy Time

My parents never married.
I never even met my father.
At first, Mom said he died in a car accident.
Actually, he left before I was born.
My mother was still married
and offered to get a divorce,
but my father didn't want either one of us.
To him, I was a love child, a mistake.
He offered money instead of love.
But Mom turned him down
even though she needed the cash.

I held my breath as I stared
at the only photograph in Mom's home.
I was afraid she would stop me from looking.

But instead of scolding me,
she lifted me for a closer look.
That's your father, she said.
He had a mustache and smiling eyes
and wore a slouched hat cocked to the side.
He was a dead ringer for Clark Gable,
the movie star. When I asked his name,
Mom locked herself in the bedroom.
His name wasn't important to me then.
All I wanted was to call him my father.

I dreamed of his photograph that night
and a thousand times over the years.
I was grown when I learned his name.

Daydreaming of Daddy

Once I got caught in a downpour
on the walk home from school.
I pretended my father was waiting for me.
That he fussed at me for forgetting my galoshes.
I no more owned galoshes
than had a father who cared if I stayed dry
or got home safely.

Daydreams disregard reality.
Imaginings were my salvation.

My longest daydream ran a whole week nonstop.
I was in the hospital and got my tonsils out.
Complications arose, so I couldn't go home.
Stuck in bed, I suffered as much from boredom
as delirium. I conjured my father.

The two of us walked the ward together.
The other patients could not believe
that this dashing and distinguished visitor
was my father. When I got in bed,
he kissed my forehead and assured me,
You'll be well in a few days.
I'm very proud of the way you're behaving,
not crying all the time like the other girls.
That whole week, he never took off his hat
no matter how much I asked.
And he never sat down.

Not even a daydream could hold him.

Who's Watching?

Aunt Grace tried her best to lift Mama's spirits
but could not convince her I was happy.
Because I wasn't. I kept asking,
Are we going to visit Aunt Ida soon?
I didn't know Mama and Aunt Grace
had decided that seeing the Bolenders
would only make me miss them more.

I saw Mama grow sadder.
Grace couldn't sit by and watch.
She grabbed the one thread of hope
that Mama clung to and wove a vision
for a future. Grace made Mama believe
that she could buy a house.
But first they would have to plan.

That meant leaving me with the Atkinsons,
a British couple who did bit parts in films.
Their daughter Nellie was around my age.
Next to the Bible-toting, Scripture-quoting Bolenders,
George and Maud Atkinson were carefree sinners.
They were my first window into Hollywood.
They smoked, drank, danced, sang, and played cards.

The couple defied all that Aunt Ida stood for.
I felt guilty for merely witnessing their folly.
Surely, God was displeased.
I feared the Atkinsons were going to hell.
At night, I knelt and prayed:
God forgive them. God forgive them.
Amen.

Homeowners

Grace found Mama a fairy godmother
in the Home Owners' Loan Corporation,
a Depression-era New Deal program to grant
working people low-cost mortgage loans.
Mama borrowed five thousand dollars for a down payment
on a two-story, four-bedroom bungalow.
It was white. Near the Hollywood Bowl.

I had my first home and my own room.
Mom bought furniture on credit
and did double shifts at the studio to pay the bills.
At auction, she bought me a white piano
once owned by actor Fredric March,
1932 Academy Award winner
for the film *Dr. Jekyll and Mr. Hyde*.

Mom put the banged-up piano by the window
and planned to pay for lessons and to buy
love seats so she could sit beside the fireplace
and hear the classical tunes I learned.
Mom didn't care much about money.
She merely wanted music in her life,
and to be happy — just once.

From then on, white was my favorite color.

Housemates

Mama and I had plenty of company in our home.
Aunt Grace was there, and before long,
the Atkinsons moved in.
So did the voices,
those invisible interlopers
that haunted and taunted Mama,
arousing fears that she was too unstable—
unfit to raise me, let alone to make me happy.
I could not hear or drown out the voices,
but I saw them pulling her their way.
They were in her head,
but I suppose I lived with them too.

Luckily, I had the Atkinsons and Aunt Grace
to offset Mama's demons.
From George and Maud Atkinson,
I gained a love for film.
George once showed me Joan Bennett
on the cover of a Hollywood magazine
and said I resembled her, only younger.
Aunt Grace took me to the movies
with George and Maud.
Aunt Grace said I might be a star one day.
She truly believed it.
Grace gave me dreams.

From Wonderland to Oz

Like Alice, I escaped through the looking glass,
or at least in it. I amused myself dancing and making faces;
my mirror image, the ideal mimic.
Was she also me, I wondered, or an exact replica?
The line between reflection and reality blurred.

Whenever I could, I retreated to the land of make-believe.
I hung on every word of *The Lone Ranger* radio show.
After one episode, I couldn't wait for the next.
I loved pretending and led my friends in games
that I invented. We'd all act out different parts.

By myself, I dressed up in Mama's clothes and makeup:
face powder, eye shadow, red lipstick, and rouge.
In the mirror, I saw Jean Harlow, the screen siren.
But when I showed Mama and her friends,
they laughed out loud as if I were a clown.

I broke into tears. Mama consoled me,
explaining that makeup was for women
whose beauty had left with their youth.
Little girls have God-given good looks, Mama claimed.
I'll let you know, she said, *when . . . to give nature a hand.*

At Grauman's Chinese Theatre,
I slipped my little hands
and feet into the cement imprints
of famous stars on Hollywood's Walk of Fame,
as if trying on celebrity for size.

For me, the silver screen
was like a massive mirror.
I could not see my reflection,
but I did glimpse my dreams.
Like movies, they were larger than life.

When I saw Judy Garland in *The Wizard of Oz,*
I sat in a trance after the closing credits.
I wondered if there were a yellow-brick road,
a wizard who granted wishes,
a rainbow somewhere for me.

Like a mirror shattering, the spell
was broken when my worried mother arrived.
Mama yanked me back to the shifting ground
of her grasp of reality and her grip on emotion,
a land more surreal than Oz and Wonderland combined.

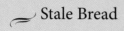 Stale Bread

Until Aunt Grace, no one had ever
stroked my hair or cheek.
She was my make-believe aunt,
but her loving touch was real.
She held our household together
when Mama was falling apart.
Even though the only luck Grace had
was bad, she looked after Mama and me.
When Mama's spells went from bad to worse,

Aunt Grace took me out. Sometimes we'd have
only a half-dollar for food a week.
We'd stand in line for hours at Holmes Bakery
to buy a twenty-five-cent sack of old bread.
I'd look up at Aunt Grace and she'd tell me
not to worry: I was going to be beautiful.
Dinner was stale bread and milk,
but Aunt Grace's words were delicacies —
cream puffs in my imagination.

Mama's Meltdown

Homeownership came at a price.
With mounting debt, Mama worked six days
a week, often double shifts, cutting sections
of negatives that studio editors marked.
Consolidated Studios, the leading film lab
and processor, occupied a cement building
with thick walls, few windows, and no air-conditioning.
Long hours and low pay but steady income.
The tedious work strained not only Mama's eyesight
but also her emotional footing. She was bound
to fall, and no one knew when.

I was settling into second grade at Selma Elementary
when a letter arrived for Mama. Her only son,
Jackie — my teenage brother — had died.
Kidney failure due to TB. Mama turned on me:
Why wasn't it you? Why wasn't it you?
I only know that afterward Mama said she heard
Jackie calling her outside to play.
Soon after that blow came news
that Mama's grandfather Tilford hanged himself.
Lost his mind just like his daughter Della,
Mama's mother, and of course Mama herself.

Mama claimed she saw her grandfather in our house.
The voices had conjured visions.
There was no denying that Mama was sick.
Grace was so worried
that she asked Aunt Ida to call me.
Aunt Ida asked me if I wanted to come back
and said that Daddy would come get me.
That would be best, she said.
I told her I had to get permission.
When I asked Aunt Grace, she was furious.
She called Aunt Ida and blessed her out.

Mama finally snapped in mid-1934.
I remember she had a seizure on the sofa
and was kicking and yelling.
She swore someone on the stairs was trying to kill her.
I remember hearing a thud during breakfast.
Mama had fallen down the stairs.
She was screaming and laughing — out of her head.
The grown-ups told me to stay in the kitchen.
The police came. I peeped. An ambulance took her
to Norwalk Hospital — the state mental institution.
At thirty-two, Mama was diagnosed paranoid schizophrenic.

What About Me?

Mama's home was now the state sanitarium.
Mine needed to be determined.
There was no telling how long Mama would be gone —
or if she would ever be able to care for me again.
Aunt Grace ignored her friends' warnings
that I was a mental case and filed for legal guardianship.
Then she arranged for me to stay in my home
under the Atkinsons' care.
I kept asking where my mama was
and when she was coming home.
Aunt Grace said, *Your mommy is gone.*
She's not going to be back for a long time.
But I'm here for you now.

Aunt Grace was convinced

that I had that special something to be a star.

She taught me diction and manners

and how to curtsy and turn on the charm.

I had blue eyes, blond curls, and pouty lips.

Aunt Grace dressed me in precious little outfits

and brought me to work with her at Columbia Pictures'

film library. I was auditioning even then.

Aunt Grace had me strut and strike a pose.

Show them how pretty you are, Norma, she'd say.

Just like Jean Harlow.

Every chance she got, Aunt Grace mentioned me

in the same breath as the screen legend.

Los Angeles Orphans Home Society, September 13, 1935

For a time, my home was in Aunt Grace's heart.
Then something happened.
I'm not sure what caused it.
Could have been that Aunt Grace thought
the Atkinsons were mistreating me,
or that they decided to return to England.
It could have been that I did not get along
with Aunt Grace's husband, Doc Goddard,
who was ten years younger than she.
It could have been that Doc put his foot down
when he got tired of my tantrums and outbursts
and decided that Grace should mother
his daughter, Bebe, instead.
It could have been that the house was too full
and that I was one more mouth to feed
and Grace was not about to risk
her fourth marriage and wind up alone again.
All I know is that Aunt Grace and I went for a walk
and she told me I had to go to the orphanage.
Just for a little while.
I can be a good girl, I cried.
Please don't send me away.
But Aunt Grace had her mind made up.

She packed my clothes in a small suitcase
and a shopping bag and told me
to get in her car. She drove
for a long time, looking straight ahead,
not saying a word.
We reached a two-story brick building.
I lugged my suitcase up the steps
to the entrance. Then I saw the sign —
Los Angeles Orphans Home Society.
I broke out in a cold sweat;
I could hardly breathe.
I'm not an orphan, I cried.
My mother's not dead. She's sick.
Aunt Grace dragged me inside.
I felt betrayed. Heartbroken.
But most of all empty.
I was nine years old, and my world crumbled.
I was really alone.
Years later, I learned that Grace cried
that whole morning.

Naked Before God

With Aunt Grace's strong faith to follow,
I turned to God. Aunt Grace told me about Him.
Said He loved me and watched over me.
When I cried at night, God held me.
I drew a picture of Him — a cross
between Aunt Grace and Clark Gable.
I could imagine the heavenly Father,
but not even in daydreams
could I fathom feeling loved.
Noticed, perhaps, but never parented or loved.
At most, I dreamed that someone would see me,
maybe even call my name.
All eyes would surely be on me if I did not fight
the urge that always overcame me in church.
As the organ played and the congregation sang,
I clenched my teeth and sat on my hands
and begged God to stop me from undressing,
from shedding the faded blue uniform
to stand naked before Him.
The only one who cared.

Recurring Daydream

Instead of the orphanage's gingham uniform,
I am wearing a hoopskirt and no undergarments.

(Jean Harlow, the actress whom Aunt Grace
idolized, never wore underwear either.)

At church, the parishioners lie on their backs
in the aisles. I walk over them.

They are looking up my skirt.
Finally, they notice.

Los Angeles Orphans Home Society (1935–1937)

For a year and a half, I lived with sixty children,
twenty-five girls and thirty-five boys
aged six to fourteen — twelve to a room.
Between chores — doing laundry, washing dishes,
scrubbing floors, and cleaning toilets —
there were trips to the beach, the circus,
the Griffith Park Observatory, and the RKO film lot.
We even had holiday parties, Christmas presents,
and pocket change for candy.

But the sweets and day trips did not make
my nights any less lonely.
I'd wake up and think I was dead.
From my window, I could see
the RKO Radio Pictures sign
like a beacon in the night.

It reminded me of my mother —
the day she took me to work
and the way that wet film and glue
smelled as the workers spliced.
I hated not only the odor
but also the RKO sign glowing at night.
I needed someone to hold me,
to tell me my death was just a nightmare.
How far from my mother that sign made me feel.

Often I'd pass time imagining that I was special,
a stunning beauty gowned for spotlights.
I scripted lines for my admirers — characters
playing onlookers in my daydream.
I voiced all the parts, complimenting myself
and basking in the praise.

My Saving Grace

Though my mother was in a mental institution
and I was in the orphans' asylum,
at least I had a guardian in Grace.
She visited every week, bringing presents
and new outfits. Sometimes we went to movies.
One day you'll be just like Shirley Temple.
Just wait and see.

Ida and Wayne Bolender, my first foster parents,
visited too. Ida brought homemade cookies
and hand-me-down clothes
from my foster sisters. I told her,
I aim to be the next Shirley Temple.

Fearing that Ida saw dollar signs in my talent and looks,
Grace forbade the Bolenders to see me.
In June 1937, Grace rescued me from my misery
and took me back home to live with her
and her husband, Doc.
He drank too much and gave me a French kiss.
Within six months, Grace was packing my bag again —
this time to live with my aunt Olive Monroe.

Olive's Branch of the Family Tree

Olive had married my mother's brother Marion.
In 1923 he had left her with three children
and a live-in mother who tried her patience
day in and day out. Olive could not really afford
to take me in. But blood was thicker than water.
At least that's what Grace had counted on.
Though I was kin, I did not feel the family ties.
To them, I was another mouth to feed.
I was so sad and scared that I made myself sick.
Some days, I couldn't eat.
Or when I ate, I would throw up.
I was eleven and had never felt so alone.
Olive's sympathy was in shorter supply
than jobs during the Great Depression.
I was last in line for everything:
breakfast, playtime, bath time. Love.
My branch of this family tree was dead.

A Half Sister, My Whole Heart

I have my mother, Gladys, to thank
for connecting me with Berniece, my half sister.
My birth father didn't want a thing to do with me,
but he wrote to Gladys in the asylum,
wanting to pick up where they had left off.
Wearing a nurse's uniform, Gladys escaped
the sanitarium hoping to rendezvous with her lost love.
He never showed up at the agreed-upon spot,
and hours later Mama was found
wandering aimlessly down the street.
Downcast, Gladys appealed to Grace
to get her out of the asylum.
But Aunt Grace knew better.
So Gladys sought help from her daughter Berniece,
by then a newlywed living in Pineville, Kentucky.
Gladys's letter shocked Berniece.

Not only was her mother —
whom she presumed dead — still alive,
but she had a twelve-year-old daughter — me.
Gladys's letter listed addresses for Grace and me.
Berniece wrote Grace and she told me
that I had a half sister who was nineteen.
I wrote Berniece a letter signed, *Your sister,*
and I enclosed a photograph.
Berniece replied with a letter and a picture
of herself. From afar, we became fast friends.
Gladys had abandoned us both,
splintering our family,
but now we had each other.
In sisterhood, we found strength;
finally, an answer to my prayers.

Worth the Trouble

When I wasn't in the orphanage
or with Aunt Grace or Aunt Olive,
I lived with nine foster families.
For their troubles they got paid.
Five dollars a week.

In and Out: Foster Families

There was the foster home where I got scolded
for wasting five gallons of water by flushing the toilet.
Like money down the drain, I was always a liability.

The family that lined up the children on Saturday night
to bathe, one after another, in the same dirty water.
It turned grimy gray. I was always last.

The families' own children came first.
Their toys and clothes told me those children were favored
and would be believed even when fibbing. I was always the liar.

At school, I got accused of stealing jewelry, a comb, coins.
I was quiet and big for my age, but I was no thief.
I got mad enough once to pull a girl's hair and knock her down.

Waiting tables at one horrid home, I imagined myself
a waitress in a white uniform at a grand hotel.
The diners devoured me with their eyes.

Mostly, I tried not to make trouble.
I helped with chores, earned my keep.
In my orphan's uniform, I was almost invisible.

Even worse than foster homes
was the fear of being thrown out
and sent back to the orphanage.

Foster Care: The Flip Side

Even for a foster kid like me,
there were sunny days —
and not only in daydreams.
I played games, ran races, and skinned my knees.

A few foster mothers, I adored.
Ida, of course.
Also, the great-grandmother who had fought
alongside Buffalo Bill in fistfights.

Her Wild West stories — tales
of her own adventures — drew me in,
made me yearn for her to like me.
Then, her great-granddaughter lied that I tore her dress.

The old woman believed her.
Just like that: I was back in the orphanage.

George: My First Love

At eight, I was a year younger than George.

We hid in the grass, visible only from the sky.

We knew we were wrong, though not quite why.

No fear, no shame, but I was still shy.

George ran off.

Rape

I hadn't asked the first question about sex
when a roomer living with my foster family
gave me the answer I never wanted.
Mr. Kimmel looked stern, and grown-ups respected him.
So when he asked me to come in his room,
I didn't consider disobeying.
I figured he would send me on an errand.
But he locked the door behind me
and told me that I was trapped.
I stared at him and wanted to yell.

But I knew if I did, I'd be sent back
to the orphanage faster than anyone could ask
What's wrong?
Mr. Kimmel squeezed me tight.
I fought as hard and as quietly as I could,
but I was just nine years old
and no match for a grown man.
Be a good girl, he whispered.
When he was done, he opened the door.
I rushed out of his room
to tell my "aunt" what had happened.

But when I opened my mouth, I stammered.
I had barely said his name
when my aunt cut me off and stood up
for Mr. Kimmel, her star boarder.
Every time I started to tell her what he'd done,
stammering stopped me.
The words stuck in my throat.
That night, I wished I were dead.
I thought screaming might make the grown-ups listen.
But the only sound I could muster
was a whimper that no one heard but me.

The next week, my foster family went to a tent revival.
Mr. Kimmel came with us.
When the evangelist called sinners to repent,
I was the first to arrive at the altar.
I began confessing my sin and accusing
Mr. Kimmel of molesting me.
Others' cries drowned out my small voice.
In the crowd stood Mr. Kimmel,
praying aloud for others as if he had no plea of his own.

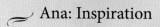 Ana: Inspiration

In fall 1938, Aunt Grace sent me
to live with Ana, her aunt,
in the two-story building that she owned on Nebraska Avenue.

She was a devout Christian Scientist.
A paid practitioner, she taught the religion
and prayed with clients.

She had her own money
from renting out one unit in her building.
She had a soft face, a warm way, and a hug for everyone.

Aunt Ana told me
that I was beautiful inside and out
and not to worry what anyone thought of me.

Junior High: Better in a Sweater

Twelve with the body of a seventeen-year-old,
I was living with Aunt Ana
when I entered Emerson Junior High in Westwood/Van Nuys.
Without so much as a nickel for a bus ride,
I walked the two miles to school. Alone.
At school, hardly anyone talked to me,
except to tease me about my outfits.
No one asked me to join their games or to visit.
I lived in a poor neighborhood,
and I never smiled. Never.

Then, one day my white blouses were torn.
I borrowed my "sister's" sweater,
which was two sizes too small.
I soon traded my white blouses for snug sweaters
and a hint of makeup — lipstick and mascara —
that I wore so other girls wouldn't snub me.
Wearing lipstick, rouge, eye shadow, even false eyelashes,
they looked like circus clowns.
Boys laughed behind their backs.

For the first time in my life, I was popular.
Other girls even took notice. Some — usually ones
with brothers — even invited me to their homes.
At my house, I had new playmates — all boys.
Four or five of them were around, talking

to me or playing games in the street.
You shake like Jell-O, they teased.
I never let them taste or even touch.

In the mirror, I saw myself in a new light.
Suddenly, I sensed my own magnetism
and saw value in my God-given good looks.
I darkened my eyebrows and wore clingy clothes.
On my walk home, guys in cars honked
their horns. I almost stopped traffic.
I leaned into the gaze like a bloom to the sun.

But my metamorphosis also made enemies.
Jealous girls, my age and older, lied about me.
Norma Jeane gets drunk and beds boys on the beach.
Even though I had told boys I was hands-off,
the scandal spread like California wildfires.
Those girls were just scared that their boyfriends
might look my way, touch me, and trigger a spark.

All my life, I had waited for my fairy godmother.
No matter how hard I wished, she never arrived.
So, with a tight sweater, pencil skirt,
and a dab of makeup, I transformed myself.
From "Norma Jeane the String Bean" to "the Mmmmm Girl."

Baby Siren

If I had a quarter for every boy who wooed me,
I would have thrown the drab orphan garb
of gingham skirt and white blouse in the trash.
Instead of squeezing my hourglass figure
into clothes borrowed from smaller foster sisters,
I could have bought new sweaters and pencil skirts,
or maybe a whole wardrobe from a store
where I'd window-shopped but had never entered.
The boys didn't care what I wore.
They made wisecracks about melons.
None of those boys got fresh with me, though.
They knew better than to test whether I was ripe.
Even if I did let a suitor walk me home from school,
even if I let him hug my waist or peck my cheek,
even if I mussed my hair wrestling boys on the beach.
For me, that was just friendly fun — child's play.
I only looked like a woman.
Inside, I was still a baby.
The bedroom had not even crossed my mind.
Alone at night, I wondered why boys wanted me.
Was it my voice, my vibration, my fault, as some claimed?
Or was it because I didn't have a father
to scare them off or a mother to shoo them away?

The Beach with My Beau

My boyfriend thought I was eighteen.
I was thirteen. He was twenty-one.
Because I had lied, I rarely talked to him,
so as not to risk sounding childish.
When he told me we were going swimming,
I borrowed a bathing suit from a smaller "sister."
At home, I practiced walking in the tight suit
before covering up with pants and a top.
On the sand, a sea of sun-kissed smiles
and scores of women all showing skin.
I had thought I'd stand out from the crowd.
My boyfriend nagged me into taking a dip.
I didn't want the waves to hide me.
So I went to the water's edge but didn't get in.
Instead, I strolled down the shore,
evidently creating a spectacle.
Guys whistled, whooped, or jostled
for better views. Women ogled me too.
That day, I was not just Norma Jeane.
I was who I was about to become.
Someone who was, for now, nameless,
but who had finally stepped into her destiny.
It was larger than all the oceans combined.

Jim

By the fall of 1941, I was feeling like a member
of the Goddard family. I made friends with Doc's daughter,
Bebe, and the four of us moved in with Aunt Ana.
But she lived a long way from Van Nuys High School,
and Grace didn't want to transfer me,
since I had found friends there and finally fit in.
So Grace got her friend Ethel Dougherty — whose son
Jim had a car — to help with transportation.
After school, Bebe and I walked to Miss Ethel's
and then Jim, who was twenty-one, would drive us home.
With deep-blue eyes and untamed golden-brown hair,
he was a tall jock and handsome enough, I suppose.
Jim had been captain of his football team
and class president in high school.
I suspected he had a crush on Bebe,
even though he took me to a dance
and a football game. I giggled too much
for a guy Jim's age to take me seriously.

When I was fifteen, Grace's husband, Doc,
got a job in West Virginia. For whatever reason,
they would not take me along. Of course,
Grace followed Doc across the country.
With Grace, my legal custodian, gone,
there would be only one place for me to go —
back to the dreaded orphanage.

By law, I was too young to be on my own.
Though Grace was leaving me, she preferred
doing so with a clear conscience, knowing
she had done right by me. So she proposed a plan:
I should get married as soon as the law allowed.

But who would want to marry me? I wondered.
Playing matchmaker, Grace shared
the idea with Ethel, who approached her son.
Jim and I got along well enough.
Perhaps because I was fun and pretty,
Jim took pity and agreed to marry me.
I found him boring but he was polite.
Grace said he'd make a good husband.
I really didn't have much choice:
it was either ward of the state or child bride.
Grace had me tell Jim that my parents never married
so he wouldn't find out later and back out.
In the middle of my sophomore year,
I left high school — to learn to be a wife, I said.
I had never seen a marriage that worked.
Unless you count movie romances.

On June 19, 1942, three weeks after turning sixteen,
I descended the winding staircase at a friend's home.
Grace had chosen the movie-like venue.
I wore a long-sleeved embroidered lace gown
that Aunt Ana designed. She attended the ceremony.
Grace, by then in West Virginia, did not.
My mother, Gladys, wasn't there either.
My first "parents," Ida and Wayne Bolender, came,
as did my foster siblings and a few other foster mothers.
That day, you never would have known
I was practically an orphan. I had more
than my share of mothers
all crying as I walked down the aisle.
Even Wayne teared up when I hugged him
and asked if he'd promise to always love me.
He said he would. The day was complete.
I never saw the Bolenders again.

Teen Wife: Jim Hated When I Called Him "Daddy"

Jim and I had a four-room house in Van Nuys
that I decorated — from drinking glasses to doormat.
When Jim got home at suppertime
from the Lockheed airplane factory,
I was always showered and dressed.

I tried to be responsive, the perfect wife —
whatever that was. Except I couldn't cook.
Jim's family probably thought I was peculiar.
Rather than talking to them, I'd wash dishes.
I was still a child who didn't yet care for grown-ups.

Or know the slightest thing about sex.
I didn't have a swooning bone in my body.
The how-to books from Grace made me freeze.
To avoid Jim, I'd lock myself in the bathroom.
One night, I even fled outdoors in my nightgown.

Jim and I were more friends than mates.
We'd go to Muscle Beach in Santa Monica
and watch the bodybuilders flexing and flipping.
When Jim walked away, they flirted with me.
I'd flash my wedding ring to get rid of them.

Our major quarrel was whether to have a baby.
Jim wanted to, but I didn't. I knew what horrors
awaited children whose parents failed them.
Foster homes, orphanages, and feeling like a misfit;
always a problem and never anyone's priority.

The mere thought made my hair stand on end.

A Name to Go with a Face: Charles Gifford Sr.

Gladys told her best friend Grace,
Aunt Grace told her friend Ethel,
and Ethel, my mother-in-law, told me:
Charles Gifford Sr. was my father.
Ethel could not be sure
that Gladys was telling the truth,
but was sure as could be
that I needed to know either way.

I hunted down two of Gladys's former coworkers
and they gave me Gifford's phone number.
I mustered the courage to call the man
whose photo I had worshipped as a child.
Once I said that I was Gladys's daughter,
the man hung up. I cried. We did not speak again.
Years later, I showed up at his dairy farm a few times.
He refused to see me. We would never meet.

World War II: A Regular Rosie the Riveter

In 1944, Jim joined the US Merchant Marine.
First boot camp and then a stint
as a physical training instructor at Catalina Island.
Since it was close to Los Angeles, I got to join him.
That was both a blessing and a curse.

The place was crawling with men:
sailors, marines, Seabees, and coastguardsmen.
Jim got jealous when the other men whistled at me.
He blamed the attention on my clothes
even though I dressed just like the other wives.

Jim shipped to Shanghai, and I moved in with his family.
I got a job at the Radioplane defense plant in Burbank.
I worked in the typing pool, then folding parachutes
and varnishing drones. The twelve-hour shifts
doing dirty work earned me an E for excellence.

My salary wasn't much, but it was enough
to send money to Aunt Grace when she and Doc
hit hard times. I had not forgotten that they
left me behind when they moved to West Virginia,
but that wound had healed. My heart was still open.

Meeting Berniece

With a wartime job in the factory
and Jim away in the Merchant Marine,
I had time on my hands and money in my pocket.
Enough for a train trip to the Midwest,
to Detroit to meet my half sister Berniece
and to Chicago to visit Aunt Grace.
Berniece and I talked and talked,
as if making up for all our years apart.
We shared battle scars, studied relatives' photos,
and pieced together our family heritage.

Berniece was not close to her father, Jasper,
an alcoholic, and wondered about Gladys,
our mother. She was still pretty, I said,

but never smiled and was a stranger
even to me — often more feared than loved.
Berniece and I both grieved over Gladys.
At least my sister had a loving stepmother.
In Grace and Ida, I had temporary stand-ins
but never a constant mother figure.
Rather than dwelling on our losses,
Berniece and I bonded with each other.

My visit was cut short, though,
when Jim got unexpected shore leave.
I breezed through Chicago to see Grace
and then headed home to greet my husband.

Picture of Patriotism

One day, David Conover, an army photographer
based in Hollywood, visited Radioplane with his camera.
His assignment was to document the civilian war effort
and portray the patriotism on the home front.
He wanted shots that would boost the troops' morale.

There was nothing glamorous about my factory job.
Most days, I wore overalls and tied a scarf on my head.
The spray-on varnish coated not only the drones
but also the crew. By shift's end, I was a sticky mess.
Covered in glue, I was no head turner. Or so I thought.

The photographer passed by me and stopped.
I was wearing gray pants and a green blouse.
He took a few shots of me in that outfit.
Then he had me fetch my red sweater from my locker
so the "boys" could see the real me. I wasn't a bit nervous.

That day and those pictures would change my life.

Still Life

David Conover's pictures of me ran in *Yank* magazine,
Stars and Stripes, and newspapers at hundreds of bases
and caught the eye of two other photographers.

Bill Carroll ran a photo lab and was the first
to glimpse the prints after the film was processed.
Bill was awestruck. He wanted me on his counter card.

He gave me my first modeling job. I posed
on the beach at Castle Rock Park near San Francisco,
drawing a tic-tac-toe board in the sand.

David also shared my photos with Potter Hueth,
an aspiring commercial photographer. Potter liked
my natural look and asked if I wanted to model.

He couldn't pay me for the photo sessions
but offered me five to ten dollars an hour
if magazines bought the photos. I was sold.

You can't take promises to the bank,
but what did I have to lose besides time?
I modeled at night and kept my day job.

Family Drama

I was thrilled to be modeling, but my husband, Jim,
viewed it as a sleazy hobby that would have to cease
once he got home. He was ready to start a family
and expected me to settle down and end my career.
A baby was furthest from my mind.
Jim's mother, Ethel, didn't help. She worried
that modeling threatened my marriage.
She kept tabs on me and passed on reports to Jim.
To escape their disapproval, I moved out
of Ethel's house and into Aunt Ana's duplex.
When Jim came home on leave in 1945,
he returned not to the child bride I once was
but to a woman who could take care of
and make decisions for herself.
That was not Jim's notion of a wife.
More than posing, I was coming into my own.

Blue Book

Potter Hueth delivered even more than he promised.
He introduced me to Miss Emmeline Snively.
She ran Blue Book, L.A.'s top modeling agency.
I barely slept the night before our appointment.
That day we met, I called in sick at the defense plant.
In a way, I was sick —
with a bad case of nerves.

Not to worry: Miss Snively said I was made to model.
At the time, I weighed 120 pounds and measured
five foot six inches, with an hourglass 36-24-34 shape.
She offered to sign me if I enrolled in her modeling classes.
My first assignment — as a hostess at an aluminum exhibit
at the Los Angeles Home Show — paid the hundred-dollar tuition.

The Visual Grooming and Professional Presentation course
covered three areas: grooming, presentation, and coordination,
from dressing the part to living the part. Students learned
how to style themselves, to interview, to pose, to impress
photographers and the media, and to achieve stardom.
Punctual and a quick study, I aimed to shine the brightest.

In class and at photo shoots, I soaked up all I could.
I quizzed photographers about lighting, lenses, and poses.
I studied contact sheets as if cramming for an exam.

I wanted every frame, every shot, to be perfect.
I was fired from my second job, though — a catalog shoot —
for fear that my sex appeal upstaged the clothes.

Still, I appeared in plenty of print campaigns:
American Airlines, Tru-Glo makeup, Nivea Creme,
Pepsodent toothpaste, Mission orange drink,
Argoflex cameras, and Jantzen swimwear.

Really, I was too short to be a fashion model.
Pinup magazines were a much better fit.
I soon became the agency's most popular pinup model.
But I also boasted wholesome, girl-next-door energy.
In two years, I graced the covers of thirty-some magazines,
including *Family Circle, Pageant, Laff,* and *True Experiences.*

My Blue Book portfolio featured several shots of me
wearing swimsuits and holding a standard prop:
a life preserver ring imprinted with the text
BLUE BOOK MODELS HOLLYWOOD.
In a way, Miss Snively had rescued me from the depths
of the ocean of my past and shown me a new life.

Headquartered in the Ambassador Hotel, the agency
also had a shady side — as an escort service
for bored businessmen visiting Los Angeles.
Girls whose modeling jobs wouldn't pay the rent
dated businessmen and Hollywood men-about-town.
I worked a temporary office job when I was short of cash.

For years, I had craved approval — from my mother,
my foster mothers, Aunt Grace, Aunt Olive,
and friends — as I was shifted from one home to another.
I always aimed to please but eventually gave up hope
of being loved. I wanted only to be noticed.
When the shutter clicked, I was.
The camera loved me and I loved it back.
All my life, I had been an outsider, an orphan.
For the first time, I realized where I belonged
and who I belonged to: the public.
Frame by frame, photos gave me to the world.

To Dye or Not to Dye

Even though my mother was rarely in my life,
her beauty advice made a lasting impression.
When I was a girl playing with her makeup,
she told me that I had God-given good looks.
Makeup, she said, *sought to reclaim youth.*
I had youth and good looks to spare.
So I resisted when Miss Emmeline Snively
of the Blue Book Agency prodded me to dye my hair.
She claimed that I'd go further as a blonde.
She said that blond hair lent more options
for camera lighting and shading. I was not convinced.
I refused to bleach my brunette tresses.

I was getting more and more location shots,
especially for bathing suit pictures.
I'd get even more work if I went blond,
Miss Snively said. Just before a shampoo ad shoot,
I ran out of excuses when a photographer
said he'd pay for bleaching and straightening.
I barely recognized my golden-blond self.
But Miss Snively was right. Modeling assignments
followed for glamour poses and cheesecake pictures
in men's magazines. Photographers gushed:
Norma Jeane turns it on and off like a sex machine.
My love affair with the camera was in high gear.

Dare I Wish? Dare I Dream?

I was the top model at Blue Book,
but no one knew that I had more
than modeling on my mind,
that I had ambitions beyond
posing on beaches in bathing suits.
No one knew my secret dream.
I had been longing all my life
to leap through the looking glass
and emerge on the other side,
not in Wonderland but in Hollywood.

If I'd had a quarter for every photographer
those days who said
You are made for the movies,
I would not have been so hungry.
I really wanted to be an actress.
I figured if I wished harder
than the other starving starlets,
my dream might come true
on a soundstage like home.
There's no place like Hollywood.

There's no place like Hollywood.

There's no place like Hollywood.

Family Drama: What About Gladys? What About Jim?

My mother gave up on me and my father,
her ex-lover Charles Gifford, getting her out
of the asylum. After scheming in vain,
she got discharged in August 1945
from the state hospital in San Jose.
The only requirement? For the first year,
she had to live with a responsible adult.
Mama stayed with Aunt Dora in Oregon.
I had never seen Berniece more hopeful.
She greeted Mama's release as a miracle.
I knew it for what it was. Probably premature.
Mama was perpetually impossible to predict.

At Aunt Ana's urging, Mama explored
Christian Science, which views prayer
as medicine. She was uniformed in white
from head to toe. I don't know whether she
was supposed to be a nurse or the bride of Christ.
But I knew Gladys was not living in reality.
Even worse, she was working off and on
at convalescent homes. Caring for the sick.
My mother, who couldn't take care herself,
let alone her children. Let alone me.

My husband, Jim, came home for Christmas.
I couldn't wait to show off my photos,

scrapbook, and magazine covers.
I had hoped he'd be proud,
but Jim couldn't have cared less.
He still expected me to quit modeling.
While he was on leave, I kept working —
until he suggested a drive to see my mother.
I was hoping that I wouldn't regret
seeing Gladys in whatever state I found her
or spending time on the road with Jim.
Mama was silent, distant, and dazed.
She pleaded to come live with me.

Gladys was more than I could handle,
especially when my career was taking off.
Sobbing, I kissed Gladys's forehead,
and Jim and I left. On the way home,
he issued an ultimatum: that I quit modeling
by his next shore leave and be ready to have a baby.
April. I did not say a word, just nodded.
I lay awake that night, heart pounding,
pondering the sleeping pills that a photographer had given me.
I couldn't muster the nerve to swallow one.
Jim went back to sea satisfied that we'd reached
an understanding. We had. I now realized
that I had to choose between my job and Jim,
between modeling and marriage.

Eventually, I gave in — not to Jim but to my mother.

When Jim came home in April,

we had an addition to our family. Gladys.

Though I'd hung a few things in closets

and staged the two-room apartment

to make it looked lived in, Jim could see

that I wasn't staying there.

In fact, I was living with Aunt Ana,

who watched Gladys while I worked.

At night, Gladys and I shared a bed.

Jim put his foot down, told me I had to choose.

After he went back to sea, my lawyer sent Jim a letter.

I wanted to end the marriage.

I'm not sure whether Jim wanted to save face

or to save our marriage, but when he got home

in May, we met to talk things over.

Jim lashed out: I owed him, he said,

for sparing me the orphanage.

Hadn't I thanked him enough?

Jim stormed out and my tears rained.

At that moment, I wanted to vanish.

With my marriage all but history, I stayed busy

modeling. And monitoring Gladys's moods.

Against my advice, Berniece planned a reunion
with Gladys. For three months, Berniece visited
with her daughter Mona Rae. At the airport,
Berniece and Gladys shared an awkward hug.
I was hoping that they would bond, but Mama
was not capable of feeling or caring.
I loved having Berniece around.
We went on day trips or sightseeing
on weekends: to tour movie stars' homes,
landmarks like Grauman's Chinese Theatre,
and the Santa Monica beach.
In hopes of reaching Gladys, we visited
her father's old homestead and the house
that she and I had shared with the Atkinsons.
Seeing the residences conjured memories
for me, but nothing moved Mama.
She showed no signs of nostalgia.

For a while, she ran errands, went shopping,
answered the phone, and scheduled my assignments —
until she soured on my modeling career,
elocution classes, and homework to mouth
words and phrases in front of a mirror.
I couldn't believe that Gladys went to Blue Book

and asked Miss Snively to drop me.
Berniece had seen my screen test
and begged Mama to encourage me.
The one ritual that united our family
was going to Christian Science services
on Sundays with Aunt Ana. I suppose
we all needed to believe in spiritual healing.

Acting was still just a dream for me,
but I knew that the studio did not like married starlets
for fear we'd get pregnant and stall
production or, worse, lose our allure.
To get a quickie divorce in Reno,
I established legal residency in Nevada.
On September 13, 1946, I had my day in court —
a divorce hearing lasting all of five minutes.
My five-year marriage was officially over.
I wasted no time flying back to Los Angeles.

That night, Mama, Berniece, Aunt Ana, Aunt Grace,

and several other family and friends celebrated

with me at Clifton's Pacific Seas cafeteria.

The place had bamboo huts, grass shacks,

hand-painted murals, a multicolored waterfall,

a rock wall, and waiters who wore leis.

In one dining room, a fake rainstorm

showered guests every twenty minutes.

As neon flowers glowed, I proposed a toast.

To the future! Even Gladys raised a glass

and flashed a rare smile. Glasses clinked.

When the Polynesian-style band

played "Blue Hawaii," I rushed onstage

to dance the hula and sing along.

The Doldrums Passed Down from Della and Gladys

If my dreams were as light as air,
my doldrums were deep as the sea.
Dark moods rolled in like clouds
and loomed like the lingering fog
that hovered over Gladys and Della.
Days like that, I didn't know what to do.
Not one stock character could save me.
Not the absentminded professor,
the antihero, bad boy, boss, boy
or girl next door, or career criminal.
Not the champion, conscience, contender,
dapper rake, dark prince, dumb muscle,
or damsel in distress. Not the egomaniac,
everyman, fall guy, father figure, or femme fatale.
Not the ferryman, gentle giant, god, or goddess.

Not the good king, grand dame, grotesque,
hero, hotshot, ingenue, imposter, or jock.
Not the loner, loser, lover, magician,
mad scientist, or maiden. Not the man's man,
mentor, monster, or mother figure.
Not the nemesis, nobleman, outlaw,
peacemaker, pessimist, psychopath, or rebel.
Not the rightful king, rogue, sage,
seeker, sidekick, or southern belle.
Not the straight man, superhero, swashbuckler,
tortured artist, or town drunk. Not the thinker,
tragic hero, trickster, turncoat, villain, vixen,
wise fool, or yokel. Hollywood archetypes
strained under the crosses that I bore.
Not even Prince Valiant could comfort me.

When I Caught Howard's Eye

All it took
was just one look
from a movie mogul
and aviation pioneer
to launch my film career.

All it took
was just one look
from Howard Hughes
for a talent scout
to seek me out.

All it took
was just one look —
a magazine in Howard's hands —
to hint I was a queen
made for the silver screen.

Screen Test

When Ben Lyon, movie star turned talent scout,
heard that I had caught the eye of tycoon Howard Hughes,
he rushed to give me a screen test. No time
to clear it with Fox studio head Darryl Zanuck,
who was out of town. So Mr. Lyon took a gamble.
He and topflight cinematographer Leon Shamroy
scheduled a secret screen test.
Before the crack of dawn on Betty Grable's film set,
in a portable dressing room borrowed from wardrobe,
I applied makeup and slipped on a sequined gown.
Mr. Shamroy lit the set, loaded the camera,
and ACTION!
I walked, smoked a cigarette, and peered out a window.
And CUT!
The scene ended without one word of dialogue.

The two men did not invite me to the screening,
but Mr. Shamroy later said my "performance" gave him chills.
Not since the days of silent movie star Jean Harlow
had he seen such sizzle on film.
You certainly have got it, he said. Whatever "it" was.
Mr. Lyon sneaked my screen test into the daily rushes
for Mr. Zanuck. Afterward, the studio head fired off
questions: Who is she? Who authorized that test?
Did you sign her? Mr. Lyon had the go-ahead.

Signed

A studio contract meant that I was on my way.
But I was underage and could not enter a contract.
My legal guardian would have to sign for me.
I couldn't wait to tell Aunt Grace.
Years ago she'd declared me Jean Harlow's heir.
Now Aunt Grace's prophecy was coming true.
But there was a catch. Mr. Lyon suggested
I change my name from Norma Jeane to Marilyn.
Norma Dougherty, he said, was too plain.
I didn't know how Aunt Grace would react.
Far from upset, she added a flourish:
my mother's maiden name — Monroe — recalling
the rumor that I was related to President James Monroe.
I now had a studio contract and an alter ego —
Marilyn Monroe. With that came a salary
of seventy-five dollars a week for six months
with an option to renew for another six months
at twice that rate whether I got a part in a movie or not.
The studio concocted a biography claiming
that I was an orphan discovered while working
as a babysitter at a studio executive's home —
a lie designed in part to hide Gladys from the press.
Ben Lyon had discovered and reinvented me.
No longer a model hoping to be a starlet,
I was a starlet dreaming of being a star.
For the first time ever, I felt golden.

My First Parts

On studio contract, I could take free acting,
singing, dancing, and voice lessons.
I worked hard too. But nearly six months passed
and no part—save press photos in swimsuits and lingerie.
I worried that the studio might drop me.
Instead of sleeping at night, I prayed and prayed.
Sure enough, I got renewed and got a raise.
I went wild shopping — five hundred dollars on new clothes.

I looked like a starlet even if I hadn't been cast.
Then came a string of bit parts and uncredited roles:
a telephone operator in *The Shocking Miss Pilgrim*,
a square dancer in *Green Grass of Wyoming*,
Evie the waitress in *Dangerous Years*,
and a girl in a canoe in *Scudda Hoo! Scudda Hay!*
That scene got cut, and after four movies, so did I.
Fox let me go. I already knew that was show business.

Ladies of the Chorus: Natasha, My First Acting Coach

I hid the runs in my hose as I rode in limousines,
frequented swanky cafés, and ate like a horse
when millionaires were picking up the tab.
At a poker party where models played hostess,
Joe Schenck, the head of Fox, fell for me. Hard.
To get ahead in Hollywood, I played the "game."
Joe had Harry Cohn, the head of Columbia Pictures,
view my screen test. He shared it around the studio.

No one was impressed except Natasha Lytess.
The German drama coach saw something in me —
something indescribable yet intriguing —
perhaps more than I could see in myself.
So Mr. Cohn signed me to a six-month contract
at Columbia. I had not only a salary of $125 a week
but also Natasha to mold me into a new vessel.
She was bossy but a blessing.

Natasha demanded that I submit to her.
For a while, I did. After Aunt Ana died,
I had no one to buffer my pain or buoy my spirits.
Natasha was fifteen years older than I,
and the first to state that I could be a fine actress.
I really needed to believe her.
She told me to know my lines so well
that I could wing it if I forgot. She taught me

diction and delivery and had me mimic the husky contralto
of Marlene Dietrich, the German bombshell.

Natasha first worked with me on *Ladies of the Chorus,*
a quickie low-budget musical. My first leading role
called for me to sing and dance. I had two duets
with Adele Jergens and two solo numbers —
"Anyone Can See I Love You"
and "Every Baby Needs a Da-Da-Daddy."
Who knew I could sing? I surprised even myself.
Fred Karger, the musical director, coached me.
That role as a stripper in a burlesque show
got me my first notice from the press.

The *Motion Picture Herald* hailed me as one of the brightest
spots in the film; called me pretty, my style
and voice pleasing, and my portrayal promising.
The studio execs must have missed that review.
After the movie's release, Columbia dropped me.
For me, the music stopped. I was blue as could be.
I stopped talking, eating, and combing my hair.
All I did was cry. It was as if Marilyn Monroe
had died and I was the only mourner at her funeral.

My only roles were in television commercials.
Natasha pulled me through dark days,

promised that my big break would come,

prodded me to keep the faith

and to read books to better myself.

Natasha turned me on to Tolstoy.

On set, she held my hand through takes,

calming my nerves time and again.

At home, her hugs comforted me.

For seven years Natasha coached me.

I moved in with her, stayed two years.

Tongues wagged that we lived as man and wife.

My need for love runs deep,

but I could not return it as fully and fiercely

as Natasha wished. I bought her a car, a fur coat,

and an ivory cameo brooch and got her a job at Fox.

She was jealous of my boyfriends, though,

and could not take "no" for an answer.

In a way, I owe Natasha everything.

She not only shaped me; she set me free.

Hollywood Underbelly, 1940s

I may have been a starlet, but not in the Hollywood
of screen magazines or countless imaginations.
Mine was a Hollywood of highs and lows,
hope and hunger — both heady and heartless.
I had a furnished room in the Studio Club,
twelve dollars a week for room and board.
There I was with beauty queens, college coeds,
city sirens, femmes fatales, and onetime vaudeville acts.
At cafés and drugstore counters and in waiting rooms —
with empty stomachs growling —
we fooled ourselves into believing
that we skipped meals to watch our figures.
Who could fault a girl for meeting men
in parked cars to trade sex for a meal?

We were easy prey for liars, phonies, and failures.
Con men posing as agents and managers.
And actors and actresses whose stars had dimmed
were almost as plentiful as pretty girls.
I detested men who tried to buy me with money.
I'd been sold to foster homes for five dollars a week.
Their belief that I had a price made me feel cheap.
There was Mr. Lazlo, who represented a man
who was willing to pay me to marry him.
There was Mr. Sylvester, who claimed to be
a talent scout for Metro-Goldwyn-Mayer.

He tricked me into auditioning at his office
rather than at the MGM studio.
As I read the script, Mr. Sylvester kept telling me
to lift my skirt *higher, higher, higher*
to show my thighs. He leaped onto the couch.
I froze as he began to paw me. Then I fought back —
punching, kicking, stomping — and finally fled
his office. He didn't even work for MGM.

Ladies of the Chorus:
Marlene Dietrich, Joan Crawford, and Barbara Stanwyck

What's not to love about a woman
who came to Sunset Boulevard from Berlin
on the wings of her performance
in *The Blue Angel,* signed with Paramount,
and became one of the original bombshells?
An actress who as cabaret singer — dressed as a man
in top hat and tails — kissed a woman in the film
Morocco? Marlene turned a taboo on its head.
What's not to love about a woman
who escaped her stepfather's advances
by leaving for vaudeville but never let on
that she was a victim? A star who evolved
from a wide-eyed flapper to a woman of substance,
with padded shoulders that made her
the picture of strength and sophistication?
Joan was a lioness who would not be tamed.
What's not to love about a woman
who went from Brooklyn-born Ruby,
a foster child, to Ziegfeld girl on Broadway
to a screen goddess to be reckoned with?
A star who played tawdry, tough-skinned gals
who worked as hard as she did herself
even after she had become a legend?
Celebrity never went to Barbara's head.

"I Wanna Be Loved by You": Fred Karger

When I met Fred Karger, a Columbia Pictures vocal coach,
even the mirror had turned on me.
I doubted both my talent and my looks.
I had almost given up on becoming an actress.
Fred helped me to find my vocal range.
And between high notes and low notes,
I found something else to reach for: his love.

Within weeks of our first meeting,
I was love-drunk: clumsy when our eyes
met and weak in the knees when his hand
accidentally brushed against mine.
When I first saw Fred put on his glasses,
my heart raced like a convertible
on the Pacific Coast Highway at dawn.
Fred took his glasses off, embraced and kissed me.
With my eyes shut, I could see a new life.

But the warmth that Fred awakened in me
exposed my own frosty heart.
I had never allowed myself to feel love
or to offer more than crumbs in return.
Tenderness was a foreign land
for which I had no map and no translator.

So we could meet before and after work,
I moved to a place near the house
he shared with his six-year-old son.
Between seaside dinners in Malibu
and nights clubbing on Sunset Boulevard,
Fred introduced me to literature and classical music—
high culture about which he deemed me ignorant.

Fred lifted and belittled me all at once.
He said he would marry me, if not for his son.
My brain, he said, was not as developed as my body.
And I was too emotional to be maternal.
He couldn't risk leaving his son in my care.
I may have been below Fred's standards,
but I realized that love is not an equation
where both sides can be balanced.
And I definitely loved Fred more than he loved me.
How much more I can't say, but it was enough
for me to ache with fear whenever he left
that he might not return. It was enough for me
to put down two dollars on a five-hundred-dollar gift watch
that I didn't have engraved because I wanted Fred
to be able to wear it when he found my replacement.
Two years after our split, I still owed on that watch.

"Golden Dreams" Calendar Girl

I had no job and was knee-deep in debt.
When I fell three months behind in payments,
my car got repossessed. In Hollywood,
a starlet with no car could not chase dreams.
The studios and agents were miles apart.
I made daily rounds at agents' offices
and casting departments to ask about parts.
Usually there were none, but I had to check.
Without a car, I didn't have a chance
of getting snubbed or of getting cast.
I needed fifty dollars and I needed it fast.

I considered calling a few rich men,
but I knew that favors came with a price.
Luckily, Tom Kelley called me. He needed
a model to pose nude for a calendar.
Tom assured me that his shots would be tasteful
and said that the pay was fifty dollars.
I at first declined and then changed my mind.
I agreed as long as his wife sat in.
I signed the model release form "Mona Monroe."
Posing naked on red velvet, I wondered
whether those pictures might haunt me someday.

But what did it matter? If I didn't get my car,
I'd have nothing to lose. I would never be a star.

Love Happy (1949)

I auditioned for the Marx Brothers: Groucho, Chico,
and Harpo. They told me this was a walk-on role,
not a speaking part. But my walk had to smolder enough
to make smoke come out of Groucho's head.
As I strutted in front of them, the brothers grinned.
Groucho remarked that I was a mix
of Mae West, Theda Bara, and Bo-Peep.
I got a bit part in the comedy *Love Happy*.

Early the next morning, we shot my scene.
By then, I had been granted two lines.
In all, sixty seconds of screen time.
Some men are following me, I said,
strutting about the office of the detective played
by Groucho. *Really? I can't understand why,* he replied.
Groucho was known for his greasepaint eyebrows
and mustache, racy humor, and trademark cigar.

To my surprise, the producer, Lester Cowan,
elevated me to a star of the film.
I went on a whirlwind five-week publicity tour:
newspaper, radio, and television interviews.
In city after city, I posed in a swimsuit
for photographers and soaked up the star treatment.
I felt like Cinderella before the clock struck twelve.
This would be the Marx Brothers' last film.

The Asphalt Jungle (1950): With Johnny Hyde, Agent

My guardian angel, perhaps Aunt Ana,
sent two industry insiders my way.
The first was Lucille Ryman, a casting agent
at Metro-Goldwyn-Mayer Studios
who saw my old screen test
and told me I had talent. She took me in
and loaned me money so I could stop
chasing modeling jobs and casting calls
and devote myself to studying my craft.
Lucille had read the script for *The Asphalt Jungle*,
a gritty caper about a jewel heist. She said
the part of Angela could launch my career.

Luckily, I had Johnny Hyde in my corner.
I may have *owed* Natasha Lytess everything,
but Johnny *was* everything to me:
agent/manager/adviser/confidant/teacher/
mentor/squire/lover/friend/protector and father figure.
We met in 1949 at a racquet club in Palm Springs.
He was a Russian immigrant, the son
of a circus acrobat. Show business
was in his blood. So was heart trouble.
He was a Hollywood wheeler-dealer,
the vice president of William Morris,
the top talent agency in show business.
I was not his first glamour girl. Johnny had discovered

Rita Hayworth, Lana Turner, and Betty Hutton.
Bob Hope was another big-name client.

Johnny claimed he could make me a star.
He demanded that I pursue my dream,
perfect myself every waking moment.
He'd recommend, and we'd discuss, books.
He also told the studio doctors to prescribe me pills
to quiet my nerves and the voices. I swallowed
the medicine and the hope that it would help.
Johnny left his wife for me and bought a house
where the two of us lived together. He loved me
and wanted to marry me, but the desire was one-sided.
Hoping for pity, he told me he was dying
and would put me in his will, make me a rich widow.
I was fond of him, but it wasn't love.
Our pairing was a deal, not a romance.

Sure, Johnny got me the audition for *Love Happy*.
But he owed me more than a sixty-second, two-line
walk-on part — even if I did get a press tour.
The Asphalt Jungle was Johnny's chance to make amends.
He took me to the MGM studio
to meet the film's director, John Huston,
and producer, Arthur Hornblow. I looked the part,
they said. The day I returned to audition,

I was a wreck: dry throat, headache, jitters.
Lying on my back on the floor, I ran my lines.
I was worried that my outfit was too risqué
so I insisted on — no, begged for — a retake.
I had no idea that I had already gotten the part.

Side by side, holding hands, Johnny and I
watched *The Asphalt Jungle* for the first time.
On the ride home, we didn't utter one word.
By the time the film came out, I had earned star billing,
but critics overlooked my strong performance.
Just as a mother bird shoves chicks out of the nest,
Johnny had thrust me into the spotlight.
That's where he thought I was meant to be.
When 1950 ended, I had been in eleven films,
and my guy Johnny Hyde was gone.
After his burial, I sat at his grave till sunset.
I missed him so much that I felt like dying too.

On the Brink of Stardom

After *The Asphalt Jungle* came a part as a dumb blonde
in *All About Eve*. The film was a backstage drama
about a Broadway star who is double-crossed
by a young actress who idolizes her
and whom she has taken under her wing.
I had a small part, two scenes as Miss Caswell,
but the first day's rushes so impressed Darryl Zanuck,
the Fox studio head, that he signed me again.
The contract did not translate into roles —

until Roy Croft, a Fox publicist, pitched me
as a pinup. That took me back to my days
at the Blue Book Agency. I could model swimsuits
in my sleep. Publications around the world
ran my pinup pictures. But I was no longer
Norma Jeane frolicking on the beach.
I was Marilyn Monroe, wooing the waves.
Fan letters poured in wanting photos, to know
more about me, and to see more of me. On screen.

Mr. Zanuck heard there were more requests
for my photos than Betty Grable's, the actress
and World War II pinup whose shapely legs strutted
to fame and were insured for one million dollars.
At a studio party, all the theater-owner guests
wanted to know the same thing: What

and when is Marilyn Monroe's next release?
Spyros Skouras, the Fox president, asked too.
He seated me beside him at the head table.

The next day, the studio began hammering out
a new seven-year contract, starting me
at five hundred dollars a week with twice-yearly raises
of two hundred fifty dollars a week.
An order went out to cast me in every film
calling for a sexy blonde: Harriet the secretary
in *As Young as You Feel*; Bobbie Stevens, towel-draped
in a shower scene in *Love Nest*; Joyce Mannering
in a swimsuit hunting rich men in *Let's Make It Legal*.

Film after film for two years without a breather.
At twenty-five, I was on the brink of my big break.
I couldn't have been more grateful.
Fans clamored for me and Fox had to oblige.
I vowed never to let them down.
Mr. Zanuck proclaimed me
the most exciting personality in a long time.
But I wanted more than sizzle; I wanted steak —
the respect due a serious dramatic actress.

All About Oscar (1951)

All About Eve garnered fourteen Oscar nominations—
a record at the time.
I walked onstage at the awards ceremony
in a black tulle ball gown and with glitter in my hair.
I was introduced by Fred Astaire, the debonair actor
who danced with Ginger Rogers in nine films in the '30s.
I presented the statue to Thomas Moulton
for the sound recording in *All About Eve*.
Eve won six Oscars, including for best picture and director.
I haven't been to the Academy Awards since.

Monkey Business (1952)

I costarred with a chimp in this screwball comedy
headlined by dashing leading man Cary Grant
and Ginger Rogers, who danced her way to riches
in lavish 1930s and 1940s movie musicals.
Cary and Ginger play the Fultons: Barnaby,
an absentminded chemist, and Edwina, his wife.
Charles Coburn plays Barnaby's boss, Oliver Oxley,
whose company seeks to formulate an elixir of youth.
The chimpanzee plays Esther, whose antics
in the laboratory tempt the Fultons to test
the potion on themselves — with zany results.
They revert to teen crushes and grade-school pranks.
Barnaby chases my character, office secretary
Lois Laurel, who is too young and beautiful
to care about aging. The film's parting words:
"You're old only when you forget you're young."

In truth, the best defense against old age
is dying young. But then I'd never know
my whole self. Grant me courage to forgo face-lifts.

Film Noir (1951–1953)

Fox studio farmed me out to RKO
for the film noir *Clash by Night,* starring
Barbara Stanwyck as the reckless Mae.
The *New York World-Telegram and Sun*
praised my turn as Peggy, Mae's brother's girl.
After that, Fox began banking on my charms
and casting me opposite well-known leading men.

But only in B movies and rarely dramatic roles.
I had to screen-test for the part of Nell Forbes,
the psychotic babysitter in *Don't Bother to Knock.*
Before a hotel window with the blinds open,
Nell dons a negligee owned by her employer
and lures jaded pilot Jed Towers into a nightmare.
If only I could have played more parts like Nell.

I got one in *Niagara,* in which I shared top billing
with the formidable falls. My character, Rose Loomis,
is a cheating wife. The movie's trailer called Rose
a tantalizing temptress whose kisses fired men's souls
and me one of the *most electrifying sights in the world.*
Rose's plot to kill her husband, George, backfires.
Instead, George strangles her and plunges over the falls.

There is no happily-ever-after for film noir femmes fatales.

Blondes Prefer Gentle Men:
Joe DiMaggio, aka "Joltin' Joe," "the Yankee Clipper"

My photo is what caught Joe DiMaggio's eye.
I was posing with two of the Chicago White Sox.
Joe had a friend arrange a date.
But I refused. I wasn't interested.
Not at all. I didn't watch baseball
and thought Joe would have a big head.
Joe had good reason to be full of himself:
he had just retired after thirteen glorious years
playing center field for the New York Yankees.
I was a rising star, but Joe was a legend,
a national hero. He was also determined.
I eventually gave in. Our first date:
the Villa Nova restaurant on Sunset Strip.
Soon Hollywood's hottest couple,
we got to know each other with fans —
his and mine — watching our love bloom.
We were both under a spell that was cast
between the sheets. We were blockbusters
and grand slams all rolled into one.

Gentlemen Prefer Blondes: Lorelei, My Die Is Cast

On my twenty-sixth birthday, I heard that a plum role
was mine: leading lady Lorelei in the film version
of the Broadway smash *Gentlemen Prefer Blondes.*
The movie musical is an odd-couple comedy
where men hanker after two showgirls:
a blond gold-digger — me — and her brunette sidekick
who wants love more than money.
I felt a debt, a duty to the actresses
whom I beat out for the part of Lorelei.
The role was meant for Betty Grable,
the World War II pinup known for shapely legs.
But Betty cost too much. I was a bargain.

I wanted every frame to affirm my casting.
I rehearsed long and hard. Even so,
I sometimes took two hours to gain the nerve
to emerge as Marilyn ready to play Lorelei.
I didn't let on why I was always late.
My costar was Jane Russell, whose cleavage
almost got the 1943 western *The Outlaw* banned.
She was on loan from Howard Hughes's production company.
The press tried to pit us against each other —
comparing her four-hundred-thousand-dollar payday
to my paltry fifteen-hundred-dollars-a-week contract salary.
The press was primed for a battle of the bombshells.
But Jane and I bonded instead. On those mornings

when I sat frozen in fear, she fetched me
from my trailer and walked me to the set.

Jane and I wiggled our way through comic gags
and musical numbers in skintight costumes:
For "Two Little Girls from Little Rock"
we donned red sequined gowns with thigh-high slits.
For "Down Boy," I was sewn into a pleated gold lamé
sunburst gown with a V neckline plunging to my waist.
That number was shot from the rear for fear
that censors would deem my dress too bare.
That scene was eventually cut from the film.
For "Diamonds Are a Girl's Best Friend"—
the song that became my signature—
I wore a shocking-pink silk strapless gown
with side slits, a back bow, and matching opera gloves.

As I sang, men in tuxedos twirled ballet dancers
with tulle skirts and crowns of roses in their hair
while women in black leotards and leather
formed human candelabras and a chandelier.
The scene certainly shed light on how men
viewed women in the first decade after the war.
One line in the movie—about brainy women—
made me cringe, but I delivered it as scripted.

Why should women hide their smarts to charm men?
I dropped out of high school, but this I know for sure:
Knowledge is a girl's best friend.

A trusted girlfriend is a close second. To publicize the film,
Jane and I smiled for the cameras as we pressed our hands
and high heels into wet concrete at Grauman's Chinese Theatre,
the movie palace reigning over the Hollywood Walk of Fame.
Gentlemen Prefer Blondes cemented my stardom.
At the time, the film was Fox's highest grossing ever.
I expected to reap the benefits: a raise, some respect,
or the right to decide which parts I played. No such luck.
Rather than rescuing me from the mire of sexpot roles,
fame was an ironclad shovel digging a deeper rut.

Calendar Girl, 1952: A Very Good Year

The nude photos I'd posed for when I didn't have a dime
resurfaced just when I had a studio contract and steady work.
When they were first published, in 1951, Marilyn Monroe
was neither a household name nor a familiar face.
No one connected the nude pinup to me.
The very next year, with my fame spreading,
the calendar was held over as if by popular demand.
Panicked Fox studio execs smelled trouble
and called me on the carpet. I was ready. I knew
the photos flouted the industry's strict moral clauses.
I confessed my "sin" and offered to face the fire — the press.

When an interviewer asked why I did it, I blamed hunger.
When asked what I had on, I quipped, *The radio
and Chanel No. 5.* I stage-managed the scandal
by opening up about my heartbreaking childhood
and my struggle as a starlet. The story ran nationwide.
Fans forgave me and shot my star into the stratosphere.
Next, a photo shoot for *Life*; I was on the magazine's cover
April 7, 1952, bare-shouldered in a fetching white dress.
Inside, the camera captured me in crop top and jeans,
lifting barbells and playfully doing a handstand.
I had everything to celebrate. Almost.

How to Marry a Millionaire (1953)

The calendar scandal broke just after I met
Joe DiMaggio. Maybe my photo teased him.
Attraction aside, we were mismatched from the start.
Joe guarded his privacy. I courted the limelight.

I was riding the crest of the nude calendar photos
when Fox cast me as Pola in *How to Marry a Millionaire*.
My costars were Betty Grable and Lauren Bacall.
As a trio of blond models on a mission to marry rich,
we rent a fancy New York apartment and court men
who, at first blush, seem good catches but turn out
to be creeps and con men. In the end, we find husbands
and learn that true love is itself a treasure.
My character is nearsighted but won't wear glasses
in public for fear that men will not look at her twice.
What difference did glasses make? Isn't love blind?

Launching *Playboy* (December 1953)

Like cats, nude photos have nine lives.
The shots that I was paid fifty dollars for
as a starving starlet twice appeared
in calendars and threatened my budding career.
But I turned what could have been a ruin
into a reward. And I prayed that was the last act.
Then, two years later, the photos, like a phoenix,
rose again — this time in the very first issue
of a new men's magazine called *Playboy*.
Hugh Hefner, the publisher and founder,
bought the photos for five hundred dollars
and ran them as the magazine's centerfold —
a spot reserved for "Sweetheart of the Month."
A fully clothed photo of me graced
the magazine's cover along with the teaser
FIRST TIME in any magazine FULL COLOR
the famous MARILYN MONROE NUDE.
The article inside cited my statistics and said
that my three dimensions fueled box office
better than much ballyhooed 3-D movies.
The writer called me *the juiciest morsel to come out*
of the California hills since . . . the navel orange.
Those four-year-old photos showed *my* navel
and more. At newsstands, fifty thousand copies
of *Playboy* magazine's inaugural issue
sold out in no time. Like hotcakes.

The Gold Rush: *River of No Return* (1954)

My character, Kay, a saloon singer, was froth
and the plot was sloppy. Otto Preminger,
the director, didn't care for the script either.
But we both had studio contracts and no choice
but to do as Fox executives ordered.
So we waded into *River of No Return*.
I played the wife of a horse thief who cheated
in a poker game and won a mining claim.
Rory Calhoun played my husband, Harry.
We are helped by a farmer and his son.
The four of us trek through the Canadian Rockies
and raft upriver, risking attack.
The film's title almost proved prophetic.
I did my own stunts, riding not only horses
but also treacherous whitewater rapids.
I twisted my ankle and nearly drowned twice.
When I wasn't risking my life, I was a prop.
I strummed guitar and sang four songs —
one atop an upright piano while men howled.
I am not a gambling woman, but I bet
no Wild West saloon ever witnessed the likes
of me crooning "I'm Gonna File My Claim."
The action-packed western was a huge hit,
and Marilyn Monroe was box office gold.

No Pink Tights But a Gold Band

After nearly drowning in the rapids
to turn a grade-Z cowboy movie
into a blockbuster, I deserved better
from Fox than *The Girl in Pink Tights*,
a flop Broadway musical turned film
whose title screamed "dumb blonde"
and that studio head Darryl Zanuck
tried to pass off as made for Marilyn.

I was proud to be a comedienne,
but I could do more than wiggle and giggle.
I hungered for meatier roles like Julia
in *Bury the Dead*, Gretchen in *Faust*, and Teresa
in *Cradle Song*. So I asked to see the script
before deciding to don pink tights as Jenny.
Then I heard Frank Sinatra would costar
and earn more than three times my salary.

Enough was enough. I was neither dumb
nor blond. Nor was I Marilyn Monroe.
I was Norma Jeane, a brunette with a brain.
My photographer friend Milton Greene
said I could seize some control if I formed
my own production company. Then I could
choose my own films and my own roles.

While lawyers laid groundwork for that venture,
I staged a one-woman strike against *Pink Tights.*
Rather than sulking in Hollywood, I joined
my beau, Joe DiMaggio, in San Francisco.
Like the company that I planned to form,
Joe was my future. At his home, I pitched in
on housework and was welcomed
into the family like a hotshot rookie.

On fishing trips and long walks, Joe and I
grew closer. On New Year's Eve 1953,
after almost two years of cross-country romance,
Joe popped the question, and I said yes.
When Fox finally sent me the script to review,
it was as empty as I had feared. I refused
the part, and Fox suspended me without pay.
I informed the studio of my marriage plans.

Seeking privacy, Joe and I decided
to marry at San Francisco's City Hall.
But the studio leaked our plans,
and we were greeted by a crowd and cameras.
On January 14, 1954, we tied the knot
in a three-minute ceremony. Beyond our vows,
I made Joe promise to put flowers on my grave
each week if I died before him. He agreed.

Second Honeymoon in Asia, 1954

After honeymooning in coastal Paso Robles,
Joe and I jetted to Japan for baseball clinics
and exhibition games. Mobs greeted us
in Tokyo. Then I got invited to entertain
the troops in Korea. Joe and I were newlyweds,
but how could I refuse? During World War II,
those morale-booster photos at the Radioplane
defense plant had launched my career.

How could I say no to the armed forces?
So Marilyn Monroe, veteran trooper,
reported for duty for a tour sponsored
by the USO, the United Service Organizations.
I hadn't packed stage costumes, so I wore
my own outfit — a glittery purple column
with spaghetti straps. Though Korea
was a snow-covered war zone, I was in heaven.

With a jazz quartet, I threw together a show
dubbed "Anything Goes." Touring military bases,
I did ten shows over four days before a hundred thousand
salivating soldiers, some who had huddled in blankets
for hours to nab seats close to the stage.
It was barely thirty degrees, but I ditched my coat
and performed bare-shouldered so the "boys"
could see the real Marilyn in the flesh.

One song's lyrics were changed from "Do it again"
to "Kiss me again" after a riot erupted at one base.
Wild applause warmed me from the inside out.
For those live shows, I was myself and I saw
my own star. If I beat stage fright, it was because
the boys in uniform handed me a victory.
You never heard such cheering, I told Joe afterward.
Yes, he reminded me, *I have.* Of course he had.

On the heels of my successful Korean tour,
Darryl Zanuck backed down.
He extended an olive branch, releasing me
from *Pink Tights* and offering me a new script,
There's No Business Like Show Business,
and a starring role in *The Seven Year Itch.*
Fox also promised me a new contract
and a hundred-thousand-dollar bonus.
I called it a wedding gift.

There's No Business Like Show Business (1954)

By *No Business,* I had perfected Marilyn,
the platinum screen dream: part sexpot,
part innocence, all va-va-voom body
and baby voice. She was my invention
and I, better than anyone, knew how
to maximize the Monroe mystique.
So I demanded costumes by Travilla
instead of Charles LeMaire, the designer
who dressed my female costars, dancer
Mitzi Gaynor and singer Ethel Merman.
I played Vicky Parker, a hatcheck girl
at a nightclub where the Donahue family,
a vaudeville act, performs. I am first seen
wearing a skimpy French maid's uniform.
It was a musical comedy,
so I sang and danced.

For "After You Get What You Want,
You Don't Want It," I wore a showstopping
gossamer gown with strategically placed
starburst embroidery and a revealing slit.
A jeweled and feathered headpiece crowned
the outfit. That dress really meant business.
For "Lazy," I wriggled in a chair while wearing
a tight black jumpsuit with an aqua sash
tied in an oversize bow. For "Heat Wave,"
I did the bump and grind to bongo drums
in a black bandeau bra and a palm print
flamenco skirt held up by a slim belt
that hid my navel to satisfy industry censors.
If you ask me, both numbers sizzled.

"When Love Goes Wrong (Nothing Goes Right)"

In baseball, Joe hit whatever came his way.
But off the field, my groom was just an ordinary Joe.
He didn't care at all for art and culture.
He was content staying home, smoking and drinking
in our rented cottage in Beverly Hills.
But he was jealous of his famous wife.
The very traits that attracted Joe to me
shamed his strict Italian family
and made him pressure me to change.
Joe wanted me to tone down the sex appeal
and turn away from Hollywood to play a housewife.
I wanted a leading man to squire me around town.
The brooding sort, Joe'd go days without talking to me.
Before we got married, I ignored the warning signs.
For the 1953 Photoplay awards, I borrowed
the flimsy gold gown from *Gentlemen Prefer Blondes*
and wore it with nothing underneath.
Slinking to the podium as the Fastest Rising Star,
I stole the show. The audience erupted
and a comedian whistled atop a table.
Hollywood's old guard shuddered at the commotion.

Joe would have too, if he had agreed to escort me.

The two of us couldn't have been more different.

Joltin' Joe had hammered his last home run,

but Marilyn was just stepping up to the plate.

I could not retreat to the sidelines, to being Norma Jeane.

Nine innings were to Joe as the nine Muses were to me.

I needed culture that toned my mind like a muscle.

Every day I strove to prove that I was not a fake.

Joe had lived up to his title as Most Valuable Player.

During his all-star career, the Yankees won

nine World Series. His record-setting fifty-six-game

hitting streak is the longest in baseball history.

Our marriage was not nearly as enduring.

After nine months, Joe and I divorced.

I cited grounds of mental cruelty. We parted

as friends. Joe has never failed me or folded.

Seven years have passed and he's still trying

to win me back. Who knows?

He might succeed someday.

Never count the Yankee Clipper out.

Seven Year Itch: Nine Months Hitched

A gust of air
up my pleated skirt.
Talk about the way to flirt!

That movie still,
a hard pill for Joe to swallow.
And for me,
a tough act to follow.

A subway grate
sealed my fate.
It cost me, though;
I lost my Joe,
my beau, my mate.

Fantasy: The Girl Upstairs (1955)

The blast of air through a subway grate
blew up my skirt and my marriage all at once.
The steamy scene was staged not for the film itself
but for a towering billboard to plug the comedy.

In *The Seven Year Itch,* I played a sultry model.
She catches the eye and the imagination
of Richard, a married neighbor whose wife
and son are out of town vacationing in Maine.

Meanwhile, New York City is under a heat wave.
Temperatures and temptation are on the rise
in the apartment building that Richard and I
both call home. Clueless to her own allure,

my character — so hot that she refrigerates
her underwear — has designs only on Richard's
air-conditioning, not on him. As if a prop, she
is nameless, listed in the credits as "The Girl."

Her fifty-two-foot likeness overlooked Times Square.

I Got Rhythm (1955): Ella Fitzgerald

Thanks to voice lessons, I overcame stuttering,
learned to carry a tune and to deliver the goods
with dramatic gestures and a throaty mezzo-soprano.
But I had no delusions about my talent.
I was not a singer who could act;
I was an actress who sang in movies.
I bowed down to jazz royalty like Ella Fitzgerald.
My vocal coach told me to buy all of Ella's recordings
of Gershwin's songs and listen to them a hundred times.
Some of her styling rubbed off, and I became a fan.

In 1955, Ella wanted to play at the Mocambo on Sunset Strip.
The nightspot's clientele was a who's who of Hollywood.
When the owner refused to book Ella because of her race,
I pressed him and promised to sit up front every night
if he booked her right away. The press would go wild, I said.
The owner seized the chance for publicity.
Amid live cockatoos, macaws, seagulls,
pigeons, and parrots in glass cages along the walls,
Ella, America's songbird, opened at the Mocambo.
And I had the best table in the house.

My friend Ella never played at small jazz clubs again.

I Move to New York

By 1954, Marilyn Monroe was the biggest star on earth.
The press overexposed her, fans mobbed her,
police guarded her, and the studio treated *me*
like property. To Fox, I was a sex machine
to stick in a niche. I had no say over scripts
and could be on radio, TV, or the stage *only* if Fox
loaned me out. All I could do was churn out hits
until the studio system spit me out for good.

Appearing in one sexpot role after another,
like little more than an indentured servant,
and my paydays were a fraction of my peers'.
Hard work had transformed me into Marilyn:
weight lifting to tone my famous figure,
dentistry to correct my overbite, plastic surgery
to soften my chin and fix a bump in my nose,
a razor to my hairline to frame my heart-shaped face,

and daily hair and makeup sessions to attain
the look even when I didn't feel the part —
plus acting, voice, singing, and dancing lessons.
And what did that dedication get me?

Typecast as a sex object. I wanted to adapt
Russian novelist Fyodor Dostoyevsky's
novel *The Brothers Karamazov* to the screen.
I would play Grushenka, who amuses herself

with a father-son rivalry for her affections.
But studio execs scoffed at the notion.
Marilyn Monroe was their golden girl;
I was imprisoned inside her and inside
the stock characters she was slotted for.
When Fox handed me another ridiculous script,
I scrawled TRASH on the front and returned it.
A telegram demanded that I report to work.

I ignored the order. Then came bullying — calls
from my agents, Fox lawyers, and Mr. Zanuck himself.
I had no intention of replying or of complying.
After undergoing surgery on my womb,
I donned sunglasses and a black wig
and boarded a plane to move to New York.
I traveled under a pseudonym — Zelda Zonk.

Don't Judge a Book by Its Cover

The brain is wider than the sky.
— Emily Dickinson

I want three things:
to have a baby,
to know my father,
and to continuously improve.
Only the latter seems within reach.
I only finished tenth grade,
but I never stopped wanting to know more.
So many questions — about my parents, my performance
on screen and in relationships, and about the world.
Books hold at least some answers.
Even though I struggle to read —
a studio doctor said I'm dyslexic —
I have a personal library of 430 volumes:
books, not diamonds, are my best friends.

The Roman philosopher Cicero said,
A room without books is like a body without a soul.

My prized collection might shock many.
Poetry by Aragon, Blake, Browning,
Burns, Jeffers, Milton, Pope, Shakespeare,
Shelley, Wilde, and Wordsworth.
The intense lyrics of Federico García Lorca,

Edgar Allan Poe, and Rainer Maria Rilke.
Plays by D. H. Lawrence, Eugene O'Neill,
Tennessee Williams, George Bernard Shaw,
and Henry James. Art books about Gauguin
and Max Weber. Five books by Sigmund Freud,
the father of psychoanalysis. Biographies
of Michelangelo, Napoleon, and Lincoln,
of composers Schubert and Beethoven,
of French writer Colette, and of Mae West,
the silver screen's first blond bombshell.
Novels by F. Scott Fitzgerald, Ernest Hemingway,
Albert Camus, Alexandre Dumas, William Faulkner,
Gustave Flaubert, Ian Fleming, James Michener,
Marcel Proust, John Steinbeck, William Styron,
Dylan Thomas, Thomas Wolfe, and Émile Zola.

My reading choices afford a more complex
picture of me than has ever been captured on film.
Oh Careless Love by Maurice Zolotow
On the Road by Jack Kerouac
How to Travel Incognito by Ludwig Bemelmans
The Unnamable by Samuel Beckett
Troubled Women by Lucy Freeman
Invisible Man by Ralph Ellison
An Anthology of American Negro Literature
The Art of Loving by Erich Fromm

The Prophet by Kahlil Gibran

The Last Temptation of Christ by Nikos Kazantzakis

Bound for Glory by Woody Guthrie

Ulysses by James Joyce

Spartacus by Howard Fast

The Miracles of Your Mind by Joseph Murphy

A Prison, a Paradise by Loran Hurnscot

The Magic of Believing by Claude M. Bristol

Peace of Mind by Joshua Loth Liebman

Forever Young, Forever Healthy by Indra Devi

The Open Self by Charles Morris

Hypnotism Today by Leslie M. LeCron and Jean Bordeaux

The Woman Who Was Poor by Léon Bloy

The Boston Cooking-School Cook Book by Fannie Farmer

The Wise Garden Encyclopedia

The Forest and the Sea by Marston Bates

Pet Turtles by Julien Bronson

A Book About Bees by Edwin Way Teale

The Mermaids by Eva Boros

Alice's Adventures in Wonderland by Lewis Carroll

The Little Engine That Could by Watty Piper

I live among books.

> *I dwell in possibility.*
> — Emily Dickinson

I Am Incorporated

On January 5, 1955, I held a press conference
before eighty zealous reporters and photographers
to announce that Milton Greene and I
had formed Marilyn Monroe Productions
so I could broaden my scope, choose roles
that showed my chops, and helm my own films.
The studio had other plans for me, though —
to play a stripper in *How to Be Very, Very Popular*
and a cabaret performer and object of desire
in *The Girl in the Red Velvet Swing*,
a film based on a real-life crime of passion.
It would take more than a news release,
more than incorporating Marilyn Monroe,
for Hollywood to see me through a different lens.
I began reshaping my career and redefining my image
to reap the sorts of roles, the types of men,
and the kind of life that I dreamed of.
I auditioned for Lee Strasberg's Actors Studio.

The Method and the Madness

Lee Strasberg, director of the venerable Actors Studio,
insisted that he could make me into a serious actress.
Dressed down, I sat in the back of class taking notes.

The other actors had surely seen me on billboards
for *The Seven Year Itch*. They probably wondered
why I was there. For the same reason they were:

to learn method acting from Lee, the master.
He had us draw on events in our personal lives where
the emotions approached those called for in the scene.

For that, I saw a psychiatrist to probe the depths
of my childhood trauma. Psychoanalysis woke ghosts
and left my feelings raw. Pills dulled the ache.

The Method's intimacy and self-centeredness
suited me, and I dove in headfirst, fully clothed.
My finest hour at the Actors Studio swayed

even the skeptics in my class. I performed a scene
from *Anna Christie*, a play by Eugene O'Neill.
Some hailed my rendition as the best they'd seen.

During one class, Truman Capote saw me run scenes
from his novella *Breakfast at Tiffany's*. He pushed
for me to play Holly Golightly in the film version.

The part went to Audrey Hepburn instead.

My New York Orbit

New York indulged my love of arts and culture.
I traded my ermine stole for a sweatshirt, jeans,
black wig, kerchief, and sunglasses,
and I roamed the city anonymously.
For once I could study my surroundings
without *being* studied, surrounded, or swarmed.
Far from Hollywood gossip columnists,
pushy reporters, and controlling studio execs,
I was free to breathe, experiment,
learn, and grow into my true self.
I also took Marilyn Monroe on the town.
The whole world was her oyster,
but Manhattan Island was my pearl.
I loved its luster and its grit.
In those days, you could find me:
writing poems and diary notes on hotel stationery
in my twenty-seventh-floor suite in the Towers of the Waldorf Astoria,
sitting on a park bench overlooking the East River,
shopping along Fifth Avenue,
getting facials at Erno Laszlo's exclusive institute,
buying cigarettes at First Avenue Smoke Shop,
wandering around bookstores,
sipping gin with Frank Sinatra in the subway,
palling around with Marlon Brando,
bebopping to trumpet players Miles Davis

and Dizzy Gillespie at jazz clubs,
or catching singer Ella Fitzgerald at a café
near the musical landmark Carnegie Hall.
You could find me:
drinking champagne with Lee and Paula Strasberg,
planning a dinner party from table settings to roast turkey,
accenting my Sutton Place apartment with brass candlesticks,
on my couch reading Michael Chekhov's *To the Actor,*
admiring Rodin's *The Hand of God* at the Met,
chatting up literati like Karen Blixen,
who used several pen names — one, Isak Dinesen —
and wrote a memoir of her years in Kenya.
You could find me:
picking pillow fights with Truman Capote,
dining on Italian food at Gino's or Costello's,
swilling cocktails with friends at the 21 Club or Sardi's,
glittering as MM at opening nights on Broadway,
riding an elephant at a Madison Square Garden benefit,
on the Ambassador Hotel's balcony,
gazing down Park Avenue and into the future.
Falling in love with the Brooklyn Bridge
and playwright Arthur Miller all at the same time.

Living Up to My Name

I was born Norma Jeane Mortenson,

but suddenly I was box office gold,

with more titles than I could keep track of:

Miss California Artichoke Queen,

the Most Promising Female Newcomer,

World Film Favorite,

Best Young Box Office Personality,

Miss Morale of the Marine Corps,

the Present All GIs Would Like to Find in Their Christmas Stocking,

the Girl Most Likely to Thaw Alaska,

the Girl Most Wanted to Examine,

the Girl They Would Most Like to Intercept,

the Most Advertised Girl in the World,

the Best Friend a Diamond Ever Had,

the Talk of Hollywood,

a wonder of the world,

the Fastest Rising Star.

The adoration was all *hers*.

The accolades Marilyn's, not mine.

In my mind's eye, I was the girl

most likely to be found dead

clutching an empty pill bottle.

In 1956, I made the name change official.

The legal formality was less a rebirth

than an erasure. "She" had eclipsed me.

No One Malady

No one knows
I stuttered
or have dyslexia.
No one knows
I have Ménière's disease,
which causes dizzy spells
and impairs hearing.
No one knows
I have colitis
that makes me run to the toilet.
No one knows
how it feels
inside my troubled mind.
No one wants to.

Marilyn Monroe Productions: The Bus Stops Here (1956)

After an exhilarating year in New York, I returned to Hollywood
to film *Bus Stop*, the first project of Marilyn Monroe Productions.
I played Chérie, a saloon singer with a checkered past
and more ambition than talent. She is working
her way from the Ozarks to Hollywood.
She meets Bo, a rancher and rodeo cowboy,
in a bar in Phoenix, Arizona.
Determined to marry Chérie, Bo takes the bull
by the horns, but she rejects his advances
until he puts his pride aside and respects her.
Though Chérie is a sexpot, I downplayed her looks,
rejecting the original costume designs
and scavenging the wardrobe department instead.
With tattered secondhand outfits
and a hillbilly accent, I became Chérie.
Just like Lee Strasberg taught me.
My training at the Actors Studio paid off.
The *New York Times* film critic proclaimed
that I had finally found myself as an actor.
Marilyn Monroe Arrives
Glitters as Floozie in Bus Stop *at Roxy.*
Critics thought I was a sure bet
for an Oscar nomination. I hope no one
put money on it. Hollywood was still reeling
over my rebellion and independent streak.
The Academy snubbed me.

Marriage No. 3: Arthur Miller

The two most asked questions about our coupling:
How had the brainy dramatist emerged
as *The Man Who Had All the Luck*?
And how did Marilyn Monroe wind up with him?
We were introduced in 1950 by director Elia Kazan.
Our first evening together, Arthur urged me
to turn to the stage. That was how to become
a serious actress. Those words of encouragement
touched me more than all his plays and novels.
Arthur's advice stayed with me for years.
I sent him occasional postcards, hoping we'd meet again
if I had business in New York or if he gave me reason.

With horn-rimmed glasses framing his stern face,
he was no heartthrob or matinee idol; more Lincolnesque.
Of course, Abraham Lincoln *is* one of my heroes.
I even collect postage stamps honoring him.
So how did a dumb blonde with a bombshell body
land a celebrated playwright like Arthur Miller,
one of the greatest minds of the twentieth century?
Surely, everyone presumed, *he is out of her league.*

He had written *The Crucible* and *Death of a Salesman*
and won a New York Drama Critics' Circle Award
and two Tony Awards. But perhaps he saw me
as a far greater prize — not a metal or glass statue
but a trophy in the flesh. Had he seen Norma Jeane?

Arthur and I dated secretly the year that I moved east
and defied Fox studio by refusing a part.
I broke my contract, Arthur broke his marriage vow,
and the House Un-American Activities Committee
threatened to break Arthur's reputation and career.
It didn't help that his play *The Crucible* paralleled
the Communist scare of the 1940s and 1950s
to the seventeenth-century Salem witch trials.

Between his plays and his circle of friends,
the House Un-American Activities Committee
had Arthur pegged as a Communist sympathizer.
When the government denied his passport,

he missed the London opening of *The Crucible*.
And in June 1956, Arthur answered a summons
to testify before the feared committee.
I watched him on TV from the comfort of home.

Arthur asked that his passport be returned
so he could pursue theatrical business in England
with his new wife — me. Thus, Arthur proposed.
At a press conference the next day, I said yes.
We married twice, first in a civil ceremony
and then two weeks later in a Jewish wedding
that our friends witnessed. Having taken
a crash course in Judaism, I married into the faith.
I had cold feet before the second ceremony
but went through with it to spare Arthur
the indignity of being left at the chuppah.

As a newlywed, I called myself MMM,
for Marilyn Monroe Miller.

Diary of a Marriage: A Two-Headed Beast

The ink was barely dry on our marriage license
when I noticed Arthur's journal on a table.
I glanced and then read only the open pages.
I regretted it right away. He had second thoughts
about our marriage, considered me childish,
pitiful, and not as smart as he had hoped.
When it came to the shortcomings of Marilyn Monroe,
my husband sided with Laurence Olivier — the actor
who would star in and direct my next picture,
The Prince and the Showgirl. Larry suspected
that I was a spoiled brat and could be a bitch.
Even worse, Arthur worried I could ruin his career.
His words stabbed my heart; the cut never healed.
We had not yet been married for a month.
Arthur and I leased a thirteenth-floor apartment
on 57th Street. In Manhattan, I played
housewife — cooking breakfast and dinner,
shopping for groceries, and running errands.
In fact, I was such a good cook that the editor
of *Ladies' Home Journal* invited me to do a cookbook.
Between domestic pursuits, I also saw Dr. Kris
for psychoanalysis up to five days a week.

I could have lain on her couch every day of the year
and still not resolved the losses of my childhood.
No matter how many times I rehashed how unloved,
unwanted, and abandoned I felt as a girl,
my painful past still ached like a new wound.

By the time I married Arthur, I was weary
of the battleground of Hollywood
and dreamed of a quiet life in the country.
I wanted to put Arthur first and for him to fight
for me. For the first time, I felt sheltered
and I never wanted to be alone again.
We bought a 350-acre farm in Roxbury, Connecticut.
The farm had an orchard and a swimming pond.
With plans to tear down the two-story farmhouse
that was built in 1783, we hired famed architect
Frank Lloyd Wright to design a home worthy
of a theatrical giant and a screen goddess.
Wright's plan was too lavish: a pleasure dome
with a seventy-foot pool, sunken circular living room,
and fieldstone accents. We opted instead
to modernize the old house, adding a garage

and a one-room studio for Arthur.
We lived in the house as it was being refurbished.
Arthur read and wrote in the morning and spent
afternoons tinkering. To my surprise,
my husband found contentment in working
with his hands. He cleared fields, planted trees,
installed plumbing, and replaced rotten timber.
I dabbled in gardening and discovered a green thumb,
but I was soon bored in the boondocks.
Though I was wilting in fame's glare, I needed
the spotlight the way seedlings need the sun.

Marilyn Monroe Productions:
The Prince and the Showgirl (1957)

Marilyn Monroe Productions' second movie
paired me with a genuine British knight,
the legendary Sir Laurence Olivier.
In addition to directing the four-act farce,
a romance set at the brink of World War I,
Larry played Grand Duke Charles,
the stiff and pompous prince regent
of the imaginary kingdom of Carpathia.

The grand duke has come to England
for the coronation of King George V.

He eyes my character, American showgirl
Elsie Marina, while out for an evening
of light musical comedy. The prince's plan
for a one-night stand fails when she rebuffs
his passes and sips so much vodka and champagne
that she passes out. Elsie awakens the widowed ruler
not only to the fulfillment of true love —
even in a minefield of political intrigue —
but also to the folly of siding with the Germans
in the brewing European conflict.

I had hoped that Larry's classical training
would rub off on me. Instead, I rubbed him
the wrong way with chronic lateness,
erratic behavior, and repeated takes.
He has yet to direct another picture.
In a press conference with Larry, my dress strap
broke, just as my character's had in the film.
My performance won Best Foreign Actress
honors in France and Italy but got no Oscar nod.
While in England, I was presented to Queen Elizabeth.

She complimented my curtsy.

Some Like It Hot (1959)

Bang bang bang bang bang bang bang!
Musicians Joe and Jerry witness a mob hit —
the Saint Valentine's Day Massacre, 1929.
They must skip town to evade gangster Spats Colombo.
But the only out-of-town gig they can find
is with an all-girl band bound for Florida.
Band leader Sweet Sue bars liquor *and* men.
The guys show up at the Chicago train station
dressed in drag as Josephine and Daphne,
a standoffish saxophonist and bouncy bassist.

Smooth-talking gambler Joe falls
for my character, the band's singer
and ukulele player, Sugar Kane Kowalczyk,
a lovable lush drowning sorrow
and loneliness in a flask of bootleg bourbon.
In Miami, skirt chaser Joe sheds the drag
and dons a second alter ego to date Sugar.
As blue-blooded oil tycoon Junior,
he even invites her out on his yacht
that does not exist. Then, as Josephine,
he probes Sugar for her romantic preferences
so he can pose as the man of her dreams.

Jerry is Joe's worrywart sidekick.

But when he is dressed as Daphne,

Jerry's worries lift and a free spirit emerges.

The lighthearted Daphne captivates

never-married millionaire Osgood Fielding III.

He proposes and Jerry — swept off his feet —

dreams of accepting. The high jinks are sidesplitting.

Director Billy Wilder shot in black and white.

I am unforgettable in a beaded backless dress.

Variety raved: *Starts off like a firecracker*

and keeps on throwing lively sparks

until the very end. The critic went on,

Marilyn has never looked better. . . .

A comedienne with that combination

of sex appeal and timing that just can't be beat.

The film was nominated for six Academy Awards.

My performance won me a Golden Globe.

The Millers Summer in the Hamptons

To escape the press, Arthur and I retreated
to the Hamptons. In Amagansett, Long Island,
we rented residences: a windmill turned cottage
and Stony Hill and Hamlin Lane farmhouses.

I browsed the shelves at Springs General Store
and drove Hugo, our basset hound, around
in my 1956 black Thunderbird convertible.
I rode horseback and painted watercolors.

Arthur surf-fished and I waded on the beach.
Summering in the Hamptons, I was happy.
In the summer of 1957 I had every reason to be.
I was pregnant and certain that I'd have a girl.

Then, on August 1, with severe cramps,
I was rushed by ambulance 106 miles
to a Manhattan hospital. It was the baby.

Miscarriage Blues: Ectopic Pregnancy, 1957

The woman I need
most disappoints me over
and over. Mother.

The role I want most
dies inside of me again
and again. Mother.

Maternal Instinct: Timing

Every week, I'd get a letter from my mother —
usually begging to get out of the asylum.
When I arrived home from the hospital
after losing my baby, her letter was waiting.
She said I was irresponsible, unfit to be a mother.
She hadn't even heard about my pregnancy,
let alone my miscarriage. Her timing stank.
Mom always knew the wrong thing to say.

Love Offering

As a gift to lift my spirits after we lost our baby,
Arthur adapted a screenplay from his short story "The Misfits."
For me, he enlarged Roslyn, a character
originally mentioned merely in conversation.
Arthur tapped John Huston to direct
and Clark Gable, Montgomery Clift, and Eli Wallach
to costar. But I owed Fox another film first.
Funny that a twice-married sex symbol
who never liked lovemaking until after she was thirty
would be cast in the movie *Let's Make Love*.
I found my male lead when Arthur and I saw
Yves Montand's one-man show on Broadway.
He was one of the most handsome men I'd ever seen.
Yves was married to actress and activist Simone Signoret.
The French pair was elegant and avant-garde,
like I had imagined Arthur and I would be.
With side-by-side suites at the Beverly Hills Hotel,
Yves, Simone, Arthur, and I got along famously.

In the film, Yves plays Jean-Marc Clément,
a billionaire bent on swaying the producers
of an upcoming play to soften its depiction of him.
His plan fizzles the moment that my character,
Amanda Dell, slides down a pole wearing
only a sweater and tights. To woo Amanda,
Clément poses as an actor and lands the role of himself.

During the shoot, Arthur and Simone both left town.
While the fictional Clément played the role
of Alexander Dumas, Yves played the role
of a lover who I thought might leave
his wife. Our trysts in my trailer ended
soon after the movie wrapped.
When a gossip columnist exposed our affair,
Yves and Simone issued separate statements
declaring that their love was strong
and that I had been foolish to think
a backlot affair would ruin their marriage.
Simone commended my good taste
in falling for her husband. Yves chalked up
my feelings to a schoolgirl crush.
He was wrong. He had chosen his words
to spare Simone's feelings. But he had hurt mine.

The Misfits (1961)

Production on *The Misfits* started in July 1960.
This was my chance to show that I had
what it took to be a dramatic actress.
Roslyn was the meatiest role
that I had ever sunk my teeth into.
Clark Gable — the "King of Hollywood" — played
Gay Langland, a grizzled divorcé and gambler.
Montgomery Clift, who swallowed
even more pills and alcohol than I did,
played Perce Howland, a rodeo cowboy.
Eli Wallach played Guido, a World War II mechanic
and pilot who never finished the home
he had been building for his late wife.
Against a landscape of the vanishing West,
a parable of alienation unfolds in Reno, Nevada.
The two cowboys and a widowed airplane pilot
rustle wild mustangs to sell as dog food.
Tenderhearted ex-stripper Roslyn is in Reno,
the uncoupling capital, for quickie divorce.
All three men are adrift — down on their luck,
out of step with the times — and drawn to Roslyn.
Through the infatuation, they bare their hearts
to her about the struggle to remain untamed.
An animal lover, she begs them to stop killing
the horses. At the same time, the men's feelings
for Roslyn test both their business and friendship.

I inserted a nude scene in Arthur's script
to please audiences and break new ground.
My nude scene with Clark Gable did not make
the final cut. The director deemed it distracting.

Like roping a wild mustang bare-handed,
the punishing shoot on location in Nevada
tested cast, crew, and my crumbling marriage.
When I flubbed the lines that my husband, Arthur,
had scripted for me, I lashed out and tried
to have him expelled from the set.
Soon after production began, we moved into
separate suites. Then Arthur cheated on me
with Inge Morath, the still photographer
we had hired to document the production.
In the desert, temperatures topped a hundred degrees.
Near the end of August, I suffered a breakdown.
I was wrapped in a wet sheet and airlifted
to Westside Hospital, in Los Angeles.
Production shut down for ten days. I needed
more and more pills to make it through the day.
Three to four times a week, I had prescriptions
flown in by my Los Angeles doctors.
The night before my first scene with Clark Gable,
I was gripped by a stubborn case of insomnia.
He bore such a close resemblance to the photo

of the man my mother claimed was my father
that I was paralyzed. In foster care, I had slept
with Clark's picture under my pillow.
Would the camera conjure those ghosts?
I tripled my dose of sleeping pills.
We wrapped the location shoot in October
and shot retakes at Paramount Studios in Los Angeles.
I was so worn down that I cried to a director
that I couldn't face doing another scene
as Marilyn Monroe. Clark, however, was proud
of his work in the film, ranking it with his portrayal
of the dashing Rhett Butler in *Gone with the Wind*,
the 1939 Academy Award–winning Civil War epic.
On November 4, we finished filming *The Misfits*.
The next day, Clark had a massive heart attack.
At the breaking point, Arthur and I flew
from Los Angeles to New York in separate planes.
On November 11, I announced our separation.
Newsmen were so hungry for a statement
that one reporter shoved a microphone
into my mouth and chipped my tooth.
On November 16, I heard that Clark had died.
He was fifty-nine. Kay, his pregnant widow,
said that the shoot — with daily delays and desert heat —
took a toll on him. Even though Clark smoked
and drank, she blamed me for his death.

"After You Get What You Want, You Don't Want It"

Of all my husbands, Arthur loved me best
and understood me most.
He fed my hunger to hone my talent
and he penned a dramatic screenplay just for me.
Arthur tolerated my tirades and my tears.
He talked with me of life and letters
and held me when I needed strong arms.
We were all each other ever wanted.
He found me witty and alluring,
and I found him steady and stimulating,
but I never felt worthy or deserving of him.
I constantly worried he would find me a fraud.
My fear of losing Arthur made me throw
his love away. He got the worst of me —
the monstrous Marilyn Monroe Miller.
We both cheated and, in the end, gave up.
If our marriage were a song, it would be this one.

1961: The Psych Ward

I know that I need help so that I won't end up
like my grandmother Della, who died in an asylum,
or my mother, who has lived in one much of my life.
My mother swears by Christian Science for cures,
but I have put my faith in psychoanalysis.
Lee Strasberg, the director of the Actors Studio,
tells his students to delve into their past
to deepen their performance. But once I dove
into the lake of my pain, a whirlpool
pulled me under. I fought drowning, floated
on prescription pills, or was marooned —
exhausted by the demands of moviemaking
and devastated by my failed marriage to Arthur.

Dr. Kris, my New York psychiatrist, put me
in the Payne-Whitney Psychiatric Clinic,

supposedly for a rest cure. But I found no rest.
My padded room had barred windows,
a glass door, and locks on everything:
electric lights, drawers, and the bathroom.
Patients checked freedom, privacy, and dignity
at the door. The nurses were always watching.
The halls reverberated with patients' screams.
I felt different and opted not to mingle.
The ward boasted wall-to-wall carpeting
and modern furniture, but the staff lacked
comprehension of the mind's interior,
which is as mysterious as outer space.

Sick and tired of being treated like a nut,
I resorted to what I knew best — acting.
How would a character in crisis react?

I recalled the 1952 film *Don't Bother to Knock,*
in which I played a suicidal babysitter
who threatens to harm the child in her care.
I also remembered the old saying
"The squeaky wheel gets the grease."
I smashed my room's window with a chair,
grabbed a glass shard, and threatened to cut myself
if they didn't release me from the hospital.

It took four people — two men and two women —
to lift me from the bed and carry me facedown
to the elevator and up from the sixth floor
to the seventh, an even worse purgatory.

They forced me to take another bath —
even though I had just washed downstairs —
and locked me in a cinder-block cell.
The administrator told me I was a very, very sick girl
and had been depressed for a long time.
He wondered how I could work in that state.
He had no clue that the camera made me tick.
I wrote Lee Strasberg, pleading for help.
He did not come. Neither did Dr. Kris.
After four days, the nightmare ended when
my ex-husband Joe came to the rescue and got me out.
What would I have done without him?

Dogs Are a Girl's Best Friend

Frank Sinatra and I always come in
and out of each other's lives.
During his absences, I play his records.
When I returned to Los Angeles
after my divorce from Arthur Miller,
Frank gave me a white poodle that I called Maf,
short for Mafia Honey. A nod to rumors
that Frank was friendly with the Mob.
I take Maf everywhere: movie sets,
galleries, acting and dance lessons,
the Copacabana to Sammy Davis's show,
parties with literati and glitterati,
to the Oak Room with Carson McCullers,
an Italian restaurant for dinner
with Natalie Wood and of course Frank.
I even take Maf along for psychoanalysis.
Frank also gave me a white beaver coat.
I let Maf sleep on it sometimes.

I like animals. They won't tell you to shut up.
They just want love. Like I did growing up
in foster homes. I'll take animals over people
any day. I've posed with sheep, elephants,
and even a bear. I costarred with Esther,
a chimpanzee, in *Monkey Business*.
I had a white Persian cat named Mitsou.
But I like dogs the best.
As a girl, I had a black-and-white mutt
named Tippy and a spaniel named Ruffles.
My first husband, Jim, gave me Muggsie, a collie.
Joe Schenck, the 20th Century Fox studio head,
gave me a Chihuahua that I called Josefa.
With my third husband, Arthur,
I had two parakeets, Butch and Bobo,
and a basset hound: Hugo.
Arthur got Hugo in the divorce.

Secrets of Style

Swear off underpants.
Trust neutrals: black, white, and beige.
Reserve red, which the studios prefer for photo shoots,
for when the occasion demands a showstopper.
Shop at Saks Fifth Avenue, Bergdorf Goodman,
Bonwit Teller, or New York boutiques.
Pour on crease-resistant silk-jersey dresses
that crumple in one hand and slide over curves
like liquid. Look for these labels: Galanos, Lanvin,
Emilio Pucci, Ceil Chapman, and for footwear, Ferragamo.
Collect little black dresses with distinctive necklines.
Every now and then, flirt with eyelet and lace.
Favor simplicity over the latest fashion. Forgo fads.
Don deep V necklines to create an illusion of height.
Wrap up in leopard for a predatory edge.
Use jewelry sparingly. Don't waste money on gemstones.
Buy only costume jewelry. Let natural beauty shine.

Apply a thin film of Day Dew foundation in Ivory Medium.
Set makeup with Laszlo's Duo-pHase Loose Powder.
Create contours, hollows, lifts, lines, and shadows

that sharpen cheekbones and deepen eyes.
Brush on rose blush for girlish innocence.
Slather on Vaseline or Nivea to lend luster.
Layer five kinds of lipstick and gloss for a plump pout.
Paint darker reds in the corners, lighter in the center
to add dimension, and shimmer on the Cupid's bow
and bottom center. Pucker up in the mirror.
Frame the visage with a platinum mane.
Place marbles in bras or buttons
inside dresses to fake nipples.
Spritz on Chanel No. 5 and adjust the posture.
Lift the shoulders, lengthen the back,
tilt the head, and swing the hips to a beat.

Surprise with wit. Seduce with smiles.
My beauty mark is real.

The Physics of Ferragamos

It didn't take forty pairs
of four-inch Ferragamo heels
for me to figure out my famous wiggle.

Nor did it take cutting a half inch
off one of each pair (as is rumored)
to produce my signature sashay.

Salvatore Ferragamo compared me
to Venus, the Roman love goddess.
He custom-makes my size-six stilettos
with craftsmanship rivaling rocket science.
But the wiggle is all mine. All Marilyn.

Finally Home: 1962, Brentwood, Los Angeles

In February, I bought an L-shaped, one-story,
two-bedroom Spanish-style hacienda
with adobe walls, a terra-cotta tile roof,
an oval swimming pool, and a guesthouse.
It's the first house I've ever owned by myself.
Dr. Greenson thinks it's a good move.
At the entry, a Latin inscription reads
Cursum Perficio, "I am finishing my journey."
The main house has two bedrooms, two tiled
fireplaces, and cathedral beamed ceilings.

I'm still decorating. I've shopped in Mexico
for furniture, tiles, textiles, mirrors, and masks.
I also bought a white piano — the same one
that my mother placed a winning bid on
and bought for our house when I was a girl.
Before she lost her grip and swung away from me.
The piano's original owner, Fredric March,
won an Oscar for his dual role
in the gothic horror *Dr. Jekyll and Mr. Hyde.*
Every key I strike haunts me.

Rx: "Vitamins"

My doctor prescribes what I call "vitamins."
I carry vials and a syringe in my purse.
There is a "vitamin" for every woe.
Vitamin A for anger and anxiety.
B when on the brink of a breakdown.
C to calm compulsions.
Vitamin D for depression and self-doubt.
E for exhaustion or everyday emptiness.
Vitamin K for kin,
my absent mother and inherited madness.
A. B. C. D. E. K.
Take to dull the pain of abandonment
and to curb the urge to stay in bed.
Caution: Do not drive or operate machinery.
Do not mix with alcohol. Do not take more
than prescribed.
I ignore label warnings and wash
pills down with champagne.

Monro-etry: Musings and Mental Machinations

On sleepless nights, the phone is my lifeline.
Psychoanalysis is hard enough without homework.
"Alone!" is the verdict echoing in my head.
My childhood was not a playground, but a prophecy.
Even in my earliest memories, my mother was sick.

When I was an orphan, the only thing I owned —
The only home I knew for long — was my body.
No wonder it became a temple.

"Every Baby Needs a Da-Da-Daddy" —
in *Ladies of the Chorus,*
I sang that from the heart.

I succeeded not by showing promise, but by baring skin.
I love moviemaking more than I love men.
Honestly, I do not enjoy sex. I might not know how.

No one knows that I study the Italian Renaissance.
When I see Degas's ballet dancer sculpture, I am fourteen again.
At the Met, I am gripped by Rodin's marble *The Hand of God.*

Songs to sing:

"Have You Ever Been Lonely?"

"Body and Soul"

"You'd Be So Easy to Love"

"Too Marvelous for Words"

"I've Got You Under My Skin"

"I Cried for You"

"But Not for Me"

"Who's Sorry Now?"

"I'll Never Be the Same"

"Please Don't Talk About Me When I'm Gone"

I won't believe that no one is stalking me.

I can't sleep because I am afraid of falling.

I can't get up because I am afraid of failing.

What I fear most is letting someone down.

Feelings are an elixir I try not to spill.

I have become a vessel for tears.

When I cry, it does not empty.

When I stew, not a drop evaporates.

Most bridges are too beautiful to plunge from to death.

Something's Got to Give (1962)

The movie's title echoes my feelings about Fox.
This is the last movie on my studio contract.
I'm getting one hundred thousand dollars, while Liz Taylor,
with raven hair, violet eyes, and a beauty mark
of her own, gets one million for *Cleopatra*.
I don't begrudge her payday, but I want my due.
The Egyptian epic is so over budget that Fox
has shut down all but one other production —
mine. Marilyn Monroe is a bankable star.
And I owed Fox one more picture.
I picked Dean Martin, my friend, to costar
as the husband whose wife, thought drowned
after five years lost at sea, returns just as he
is about to remarry. For the first time, I play
a mother in a movie. The children who play
my son and daughter are darling, but I am too ill

many days to make it to the set. Sinusitis,

laryngitis, fevers, and a fainting spell

on top of insomnia. Not even pills help.

The studio execs think I am concocting excuses.

Weeks ago, I told them I'd be singing for the president.

They gave me time off from the eight-week shoot

and then reneged because we got behind schedule.

I came anyway. Marilyn Monroe is *my* property.

When the helicopter took off from the studio,

I saw how tiny the backlot — conjurer of worlds,

spinner of dreams — really was. The movie business,

like the bogus wizard behind the curtain in Oz.

I *will be* onstage at New York's Madison Square Garden.

I will not wear ruby slippers but a diamond gown.

What can the studio do? Fire Marilyn Monroe?

The Birthday Gift

Each bottle of Chanel No. 5
contains the distilled essence
of more than one thousand blooms —
jasmine and roses from France.
That fragrance is my favorite.

I painted a single red rose,
the national flower of the United States,
for President Kennedy's birthday,
a fitting gesture, I thought.
Watercolors funnel tears into the sublime.

I may never give Jack the gift.
How I adore roses.
My second husband, Joe,
knows that better than anyone.

The Kennedys

I will never discuss my ties to the Kennedys:
Jack, the president, and his brother Bobby,
who is the US attorney general
and a married father of seven children.

In the '20s, their father, Joe, ran three movie studios.
The industry was new, and he ushered in talkies.
His mistress was silent screen star Gloria Swanson.
As the saying goes: like father like sons.

I met Jack at a party at Peter Lawford's house.
The actor was married to my friend Pat,
the president's younger sister. Peter had costarred
in the caper *Ocean's 11* opposite Frank Sinatra,
Dean Martin, Joey Bishop, and Sammy Davis —
who are known in Vegas as the Rat Pack.

It is said that the president regularly beds
Hollywood starlets at Pat and Peter's place.
Jack's helicopter is such a fixture
behind the Lawfords' beachfront home
in Santa Monica that it is dubbed the Western White House.
That is all I will share.

Beyond that, believe what you like.
I will never tell which brother I preferred

or whether either promised to marry me.
I will neither admit nor deny rendezvous
in discreet hotels or borrowed apartments.
I will never say whether these rumors are true:
that butlers and housekeepers
found my blond hairs in the White House
and that Jack and I had a one-night stand
at the home of singer-actor Bing Crosby.
Never mind reports I called Jackie, the First Lady,
to tell her that I had had an affair with Jack
or that I called Bobby at the Justice Department,
threatening to go public about an affair.
All of that remains speculation.
I will hold no press conference
to feed fans' hunger for scandal.
Call that love if you like.
The truth lies locked inside my red leather diary.
Some secrets I will carry to my grave.

Late: A Litany of Excuses

I am late because I am punishing my father for making me wait.
I am late because playing Marilyn Monroe is exhausting.
I am late because hair, makeup, and wardrobe take hours.
I am late because I do not want to be less than fans deserve.
I am late because I want to be photo perfect when I arrive.
I am late because legends do not emerge overnight.

I am late because a constellation of talent precedes me.
On the star-studded bill: singers, actors, comedians, and dancers —
Harry Belafonte, Jack Benny, Maria Callas, Diahann Carroll,
Bobby Darin, Jimmy Durante, Ella Fitzgerald, Henry Fonda,
Danny Kaye, Peggy Lee, Shirley MacLaine, Miriam Makeba,
and the Jerome Robbins Ballet. Marilyn will be the finale.

I am late because the light from the nearest stars takes
four years to reach the Earth and twinkle in our eyes.
If I am late tonight, I am sure the audience will wait
and that the one minute I serenade the president
will be the only lasting memory of the entire evening.
How much longer? How much longer must I stand still?

Who Is Marilyn Monroe?

For photographers, I am part myth,
part muse, part plastic, part machine —
personas turned on and off at will.
For Alfred Eisenstaedt, I am a New York socialite
in slacks and top, curled on the couch reading.
For Cecil Beaton, I am the rococo-era portrait
by Jean-Baptiste Greuze of Ariadne,
looking as if she is waking from a dream.
For Richard Avedon, I am silent screen vamp
Theda Bara playing Queen Cleopatra.
For Milton Greene, I am a ballerina,
a swan landing on a nest of tulle.
For Sam Shaw, I am Botticelli's *Birth of Venus*,
in my white maillot on a Hamptons beach.
For Andre de Dienes, I am a saint crowned with thorns.
For the camera, I can be Aphrodite
or an odalisque reclining on a bed
and covered only by a sheet or nothing at all.
Doug Kirkland says that I take his breath away.

For America in the postwar years,
I am the pleasing antidote to mass destruction,
a blond bomb who rocketed from orphaned obscurity
to become the hottest pinup of the Cold War,
the US standoff with the Soviet Union.

For Americans, I am democratic beauty,
as everyday as a lunch counter waitress.
To my cat, dog, and two parakeets,
I am the hand that strokes and feeds.
To the studio big bands that I front
during musical numbers, I am a jazzy song stylist.
I am all the nicknames I've called myself:
Noodle, Sam, Max, Clump, and Sugar Finny.
I am the scared child whose mother
put her in a bag to steal her from a foster home
and the only parents she'd ever known.
I am a jet-setter with Louis Vuitton luggage.
I am the fantasy who lives next door,
a celluloid figment of everyman's imagination.

For Aunt Grace, I was the heir to Jean Harlow,
Hollywood's first blond siren.
I am the midcentury female counterpart
of the comic tramps played by silent movie stars
Charlie Chaplin and Buster Keaton.
For talent scouts and film crews, I evoke
Hollywood's most enchanting imports:
Greta Garbo and Marlene Dietrich.
To critic Otis Guernsey, I am marble
in the masterful hands of Michelangelo.

To director François Truffaut, I am a magnet,
drawing the eye from head to toe.
To director John Huston, I am the truth.

I am not made of stone but of porcelain.
I am a Fabergé egg that has broken into a thousand pieces.
I am glued together with tears.

Everyone knows Marilyn Monroe.
But precious few know Norma Jeane.
I'm not even sure that I remember her anymore.
I am a woman in search of myself.

Epilogue
A Found Poem of Headlines and Quotes

Mr. President, the late Marilyn Monroe
— Peter Lawford, actor, introducing Marilyn Monroe
Madison Square Garden
May 19, 1962

Happy birthday, Mr. President
— Marilyn Monroe
Madison Square Garden
May 19, 1962

Studio Fires Marilyn, Replaces Her in Film
Los Angeles Times
June 9, 1962

MARILYN MONROE
A SKINNY-DIP YOU'LL NEVER SEE ON THE SCREEN
They Fired Marilyn:
Her Dip Lives On
Life
June 22, 1962

Marilyn Monroe Kills Self
Found Nude in Bed . . . Hand on Phone . . . Took 40 Pills
New York Mirror
August 6, 1962

PRESIDENT KENNEDY SLAIN BY ASSASSIN
Shot in Dallas; Johnson Sworn In
Pittsburgh Press
November 22, 1963

LOS ANGELES, WEDNESDAY, 12:15 am
Robert Kennedy lies stricken by a gunman's bullets —
and one of his supporters cries out in disbelief,
GOD! NOT AGAIN!
Daily Mirror
June 6, 1968

People Poll of the Century
Sexiest Woman: Marilyn Monroe
People
December 31, 1999

DiMaggio's Dying Words:
"I'll Finally Get to See Marilyn"
New York Post
August 8, 2000

50 Years on, Marilyn Monroe's Star Power Shines Bright
Las Vegas Sun
July 31, 2012

Marilyn Monroe's "Happy Birthday, Mr. President" Dress Sells for
$4.8 Million
Actress' May 1962 dress breaks record for most expensive dress
ever, besting her "The Seven Year Itch" garb
Rolling Stone
November 19, 2016

Joe DiMaggio placed a 20-year order of a half-dozen roses
to be put on Marilyn Monroe's grave three times a week
Vintage News
March 19, 2017

The Craziest Conspiracy Theories About Marilyn Monroe's Death
Have you heard the one about UFOs?
Cosmopolitan
July 27, 2017

Hugh Hefner Will Be Laid to Rest
Beside Playboy's First Cover Girl Marilyn Monroe
The iconic publisher died Wednesday at 91
HuffPost
September 28, 2017

PHOTO CREDITS